BASTARD BOSS

NEW YORK TIMES BESTSELLING AUTHOR

LISA RENEE JONES

ISBN-13: 979-8364343468

www.lisareneejones.com

DEAR READERS:

I'm so excited to be back in the Necklace Trilogy world! If you haven't read my Necklace Trilogy, fear not! You do not need to read any book prior to this one, but fans of my Necklace Trilogy have been dying to read Tyler & Bella's story, and I'm so glad you all pushed me to write this duet because it has fast become one of my most favorite books I've written.

I'm including the chapters of *Boss Me Around* in this book just in case you haven't read it yet. It's the free prologue that goes with this story, but I didn't want anyone to miss out on it. So if you've read it, you can begin with chapter six, or just turn the page and begin reading :)

xoxo,

Lisa Renee Jones

CHAPTER ONE

Tyler

When your father's a bastard, you become one, too.

I stand on the balcony of my downtown apartment, a whiskey glass in my hand, watching the avalanche of rain plummeting the city. Nashville is drowning in rain, while my family is drowning in the disgrace and sorrow caused by my father. True to the dictator he was, he is gone now, his very absence a command that I clean up the mess he's left of the reputation of the family law firm. Not an easy task, when much like the rain now rushing through the streets below, scandal sweeps through the hallways of the luxurious offices of Hawk Legal in a bloody damn river.

I down my drink and set the glass on the patio table, and with good reason. Nothing good comes of my drinking. I can't even become an actual alcoholic, though I tried once, a little too hard. I'd submerged myself in my father's disapproval and swam around in it with such ease it was as if I was vacationing in that bullshit. I think back to one particularly nasty confrontation with my father in which he told me I would never be good enough to run the family firm I was already running.

That was the night I met Allison, *really* met her, rather than just passing her in the office hallways.

She'd delivered paperwork to my apartment that night for a big case I was managing the next morning as a favor to my assistant. When she arrived, I'd been three sheets to the wind.

She'd stayed until morning.

I'd known it was wrong. She was my employee. But it was almost as if I wanted to live up to my father's disapproval, wallow in it, even. One night had become months of involvement. I grew to care for Allison, but she'd come to love me at a time when I hated myself too damn much to even understand the meaning of love. I was toxic and I knew it.

She'd confessed her feelings for me on a night when I was out of my own skin, angry with my father, angry with myself for letting him control me when I let nothing else control me. I was on a path of self-destruction, destined to take her down with me, destined to hurt her. I walked away from her because I didn't want that to happen.

I wanted to save her.

I failed.

All I did was drive her into my father's arms.

Now a year later, and a year after Allison left the company, they're both dead. Her dead at my father's hand after, per the police, she threatened to go to my mother. Him dead after someone put it all together. That someone should have been me, but I was too wrapped up in my own bullshit with my father to see beyond myself.

To complicate matters, the entire situation is now blasted on every news station for Hawk Legal clients to hear, a problem that jeopardizes our client list, and therefore the stability of two hundred and fifty employees on staff. Also blasted on the television is speculation over whether I will attend today's memorial for my father to support my mother, who isn't mourning him, but rather serving an obligation she feels publicly. I tried to talk her out of this ridiculous show of public mourning, but again, I failed. It's a pattern, it seems, and I don't like it.

Why am I even entertaining attending a memorial that makes us all look like we support the man who did such a heinous thing?

He *killed* Allison.

Decision made, I loosen my tie and pick up the glass. I'm not going to the farce of a memorial that only makes my mother look foolish, not respectable, as she claims. I tilt my glass to my lips, cursing when I find it empty. I'm a ball of nasty emotions, the kind no man ever wishes to feel.

I enter the apartment, shrug out of my jacket, and toss it on the chair that's part of the seating area adjacent to the patio, but I don't wait to see it land. I'm already continuing to the bar in the main living area. Once there, I do what any man would do on the day of his murderous father's memorial—I refill my glass, and do so with Macallan 25 whiskey. It was my father's favorite drink, and I don't drink it now to honor him in his death, but rather as a *fuck you, you will not take anything else from me, not now or ever.* I down a swallow of the booze and walk to the living room, sit down on the black leather couch in front of the fireplace and stare down at the journal lying on the table. It was her journal—Allison's.

She left it here but told me to keep it, read it even, and maybe I would wake up. I never even considered reading it. I didn't want to know what was inside. But I stare at it now, desperate to feel as if she is alive again. I flip it over and open it to the last page, which is filled with a delicate script, and the words read: *Sometimes you love someone who cannot love you back, and therefore you are destined for heartbreak. No, you are destined to be broken. He broke me but I can only blame myself. I knew loving Tyler Hawk was a mistake, but the heart wants what the heart wants. Mine wanted him. But I wasn't his person. Maybe that means he wasn't mine, either, and one day, I hope to find the person who will love me. For now, ironically, I end this journal, on the last page of the book, and the bittersweet last chapter of my time with Tyler Hawk.*

It's as if a fist reaches up from the bowels of hell, shoves itself inside my chest, and all but rips my heart from my body and grabs ahold of my insides and twists.

The journal slides from my grip and the leather backing all but slams shut, but its words are far from silenced in my mind. I swear it still shouts at me, smoldering words of contempt I feel with slashes of a blade. Anger burns inside me with the certainty that contempt is well deserved.

I snatch my phone from my pocket and dial the detective on the case, only to be thrown to voicemail. I leave Detective Wallace a message. "I'm still waiting on an answer. How long was my father involved with Allison? Call me back, Detective." I disconnect, uncertain why I need to know that answer but, on some level, I am aware of my clawing need to find a way that this is not my fault when that's a coward's ploy.

I'm accountable for my actions and to some degree, his as well.

My eyes fall on the journal and my desperation to escape its scorn has me reaching for the remote control. I turn on the TV only to hear a newscaster say, "How will Tyler Hawk handle the legacy of the name and the firm he's inherited when that legacy is now murder?"

I curse, turn off the TV again, and down my drink.

The door buzzes, and I set my glass on the table with unnecessary force, drawing in a calming breath. I'd say whoever is here has security clearance, therefore is

8

friendly, but I just had a reporter at my door after slipping past the guard in the lobby. Everyone wants a piece of the Hawk family pie right now. I'd ignore whoever dares come to me today, but they're already knocking again. "Holy hell," I grumble, hands to my knees as I push to my feet, briskly striding to the door with every intention of making whoever is on the other side go the fuck away.

I unlock the door and swing it open, only to find a blonde bombshell in a black funeral dress standing in front of me. And not just any bombshell. This is Bella Bailey, an attorney for Hawk Legal, and agent to the rich and famous, who, under my tutelage, now represents a growing list of A-listers. She's also the half-sister to Dash Black, the author who turned an assassin he hunted when he was in the FBI into the star of his bestselling novels. Dash wasn't an A-lister when I hired his sister, nor was he my friend. He is both of those things now, though the friendship side of the equation is complicated at best.

As is my relationship with Bella.

One might call me a moth drawn to the flame, but she would be the one burned if I ever touched her. Thank fuck Dash has always stood between me and her. Meanwhile, there was Allison, alone in this world, and exposed and vulnerable to the likes of me, and apparently, my father.

"Why are you here, Bella?" I demand softly.

"Because I knew you'd get dressed to go to the memorial but never leave your apartment."

I narrow my eyes on her. "And how would you know that?"

"I learned the art of observation from the best," she says, adding without hesitation, "*you*. I know you better than you obviously think I do." She indicates the bag in her hand. "Ice cream. My favorite way to cope with every bad thing life throws my way and often the good things, too. And yes, I can eat a whole pint and I don't mind if you watch." She moves forward as if to enter the apartment.

I step left and block her entry, the bag in her hand colliding with my body. Her bright, baby blue eyes go wide, shock registering with a soft whoosh of air from her lips. "This isn't a good idea, *Bella*."

"Ice cream is always a good idea, *Tyler*."

She's one of the only people at the office who dares to call me Tyler, which I blame on her brother. Maybe those lines he drew between us are not that wide after all. "This is not a good idea," I repeat.

She laughs, a soft, amused laugh, that should surprise me but does not. This is Bella, after all. She knows how to handle big egos, big wallets, and impossible financial negotiations, and rather than a jaded mentality that often comes with experience, she manages a demureness that feels as genuine as the day I met her. "What?" she challenges. "Are you going to bite?"

"Among other things, if you're not careful," I assure her. "I am not in the right state of mind for you to play the sweet little girl rescuing me."

Her lashes lower, dark half circles against her ivory skin, before her eyes are once again fixed on me. "I'm far more complicated than that description and we both know it."

"Bella—"

"I can handle you, and your grief, Tyler, probably better than you can right now."

"Like Allison handled me?" I challenge.

"You didn't kill her."

"I drove her into the arms of her killer. She worked for me. I had no business touching her."

"As do I. Which is why we both know you're safe to let me in."

"But are *you* safe?"

"Yes," she assures me, and she pushes on the bag that still rests between us as if that little bit of nudging will force me to step aside and allow her entry. It doesn't, and yet I find myself easing away from the door, allowing her to enter my apartment. She's inside in a flash, and the familiar, sweet scent of jasmine perfume ignites a burn of desire in my body, a problem she simply doesn't seem to understand. She buries her troubles in a pint of ice cream. I'd rather bury mine in her. I shut the door and flip the lock into place.

LISA RENEE JONES

CHAPTER TWO

Tyler

By the time I've turned back around, the only sign of Bella is her purse and the bag of ice cream sitting on the coffee table.

The sound of riffling about draws my attention toward the archway to my right, which is also my kitchen. Apparently, Bella has made herself right at home, when the only time she was here before was the day after my father died and that was with her brother for all of fifteen minutes.

I follow the sweet scent of her perfume and step into the doorway, bringing her into view as she shuts the silverware drawer. Clearly aware of my presence, she rotates to face me, holding up two spoons. Already I'm thinking of her on the counter, her skirt to her waist, and my cock buried inside her.

Which really does make me my father's son, and I don't like it any more than Bella would me if she knew where my head was at right now.

I catch my hands on the curved archway on either side of me and will my blood to cool.

"Bingo," she announces, waving the spoons around. "I found what I was looking for. You're very organized, which doesn't surprise me. You're ridiculously anal. This kind of perfection would drive me crazy. I need a little disorder to feel at home. Good thing I just work for you." She walks toward me and stops in front of me. "Please tell me you don't have a problem eating right out of the pint, because somehow that feels like something someone *this* anal would not do."

"I'm not anal. I hire a housekeeper who is."

"Of course, you do," she replies, a smirk on her pretty lips before she ducks under my arm.

I fight the urge to reach for her and pull her to me, and that one-second beat that I lose to that internal battle is enough to allow her to escape. In her absence I am left with her words, *of course, you do.* I'm not sure if that is her way of saying the maid explains nothing, or perhaps, a jab at me for not cleaning my own house. It shouldn't matter. It wouldn't with anyone else.

I am *not* in the right state of mind for her to be here right now.

With a grimace, I push off the archway and rotate, already in pursuit of Bella with every intention of sending her on her way. She's by the fireplace, and with a flip of a switch, it flashes, flames licking at the glass before they settle into a warm, steady burn. "Perfect," she approves, kicking off her high heels, then claiming the leather chair to the left of the couch. "Now we're ready."

I pause at the line just outside the living room as she removes the first pint of ice cream from the bag, followed by three more, and the damn journal manages to end up in the center of the buffet she's created. With a silent curse, I move further into the room and sit down on the couch, in front of the table. I consider ignoring the journal, but Bella is not an average guest who would be polite and ignore what is in front of her. She's the adult version of the curious kid with the ability to be nosey and still come off as charming.

I reach for the journal and shove it between the cushions to my right, while Bella remains on my left. If she notices my actions, she blows it off, her sole focus on convincing me to eat ice cream.

"Okay," she says. "I have four flavors, all my favorites." She indicates pints with the touch of her hand. "Milk chocolate peanut butter. Cookies and cream. Key lime pie. And finally." She taps the final pint. "Cookie dough. I think chocolate peanut butter fits you. It's rich and complicated."

My brows shoot up. "I'm not sure if that's an insult or a compliment."

"Depends on the day and if you've pissed me off that day, which is fairly often, by your own decision to do so, of course."

She's not wrong. I push my employees to be all they can be, even when it's uncomfortable. I don't play the game of pretending otherwise. "And yet, here you sit," I point out, "in my living room."

"I'm crazy like that," she concurs. "And you have done a lot for my brother, so I owe you."

She's talking about Dash's obsession with underground fighting that he couldn't control even if the scandal it equaled might have halted the development of his books into Hollywood films. Fighting was a drug, and just as Dash once forced me to let go of the booze as a crutch, I did the same for him with fighting. I forced him to walk away.

"I protected my interests," I say, dismissing a personal side to this that creates an obligation to me she does not possess.

"And mine," she replies glibly. "He's my client, too."

"He's your brother."

"And your friend."

My cellphone chooses that moment to ring, and the idea that this might be the detective working on Allison's case has me tuning out Bella's relentless attempt to humanize me and reaching for my phone. I grimace as I find my mother's number on the caller ID, clamping down on the emotional spike that declares me human after all, I push to my feet. "I need to take this." I don't look at Bella.

I walk a few feet to the patio door and step outside again, the rain pitter-pattering, with no sign of easing. "Mother," I greet, at this point using my earbuds.

"You aren't going to show up, are you?"

"I cannot, in good conscience, go to an event meant to honor that man."

She's silent a beat that stretches into two. "Good. Because I'm not going, either. You were right. The memorial was foolish. It only serves to paint me as stupid all over again." There's a hitch to her voice that bloodies my heart all over again.

I lean on the table as if it might just hold the burden of life beating down on me and her right now, and offer some form of relief. "You aren't stupid, Mother. You were a wife who loved her husband."

"I was a wife who stayed too long. Stop trying to give me an excuse for being foolish. It serves no purpose."

No good purpose, I think, before I say, "A friend brought me ice cream and lots of it. Apparently, it's supposed to lift one's spirits. Why don't you come over?"

"Thank you, son, but I'm actually headed to the airport. A client of mine has been hitting on me for years. I turned him down, of course, but I was flattered. I called him before I called you. He offered to take me to Europe to escape the press. I said yes."

Two years ago, my mother left the firm to start an investment firm, in which many of our clients are now involved. The idea that I know this man isn't hard to assume. Protectiveness bristles. "Who's this client?"

16

"No one you know," she says. "And he can't be worse than your father. I'll call you tomorrow once I'm settled in. Take care of yourself, Tyler. And forget living in your father's shadow."

"Easier said than done," I remind her, not that she needs to be reminded. The press is doing a beautiful job of that for us all.

"That's why I left the firm to start my own business," she replies. "To step out from under his dominant presence. But now he's gone. And I've moved on. You're acting CEO but the 'acting' title is a mere formality. I have no idea why your father delayed the reading of his will for sixty days, but it doesn't matter. That firm is yours. Act like it and you will not fail." She disconnects.

I let the phone disconnect and stand there, watching the rain pitter-patter and bounce off the concrete of the patio wall. If only the impact of my father's actions were as easy to deflect.

"Tyler."

At the sound of Bella's voice, I rotate to face her. She's standing there in her hosed feet, the light casting her in a glow, her hair messed up, and I didn't even help get the job done.

"Everything okay?" she asks, tentatively.

I stand there, mentally planting my feet in the ground when they want to move toward her, aware of her in ways that are not safe for her or me. The curve of her breasts against her fitted bodice. The curve of her hips in the slender cut of the dress.

"It was my mother," I say. "She called off the memorial. She's going to Europe with another man. I think she's looking for an escape."

Her lips part and then press together before she says, "Yes. I can see how an escape might feel necessary."

Despite logic and good sense, I step toward her, and as I draw nearer, she doesn't back away.

CHAPTER THREE

Tyler

I halt close to her, near enough that I could reach out and touch her. The jasmine scent of perfume flares in my nostrils and mixes with the earthy scent of nature and rain. The results are sultry and erotic, stirring a heaviness in my body that as logic serves is trouble, is dangerous, but I'm not feeling logical at all. My cock, now pressing uncomfortably against my zipper, is not one little bit logical.

"Yes," I say softly, my gaze tracing the plump fullness of her bottom lip. I crave a taste of her, just one taste. Just one lick. But I'm not foolish enough to believe it would be one and done. I'd want more. I'd take more, everything she'd let me take. And I'd kiss far more than her mouth. I also know we'd be changed forever, and I'd be repeating a mistake that left more than one person dead. Still, I don't move away, I simply add, "I do believe I can understand an escape could be necessary, too."

I'm no longer talking about my mother's jaunt across the world with a client. I'm talking about me and Bella right now.

And when her chin lifts and her eyes collide with mine, there is an undeniable punch between us, the air thick with lust. She lifts her hand as if she means to touch me, but pauses mid-air, seems to reconsider, and allows her arm to lower. "I'm not sure there's anything wrong with that."

And yet, right here and now, escape, at least the kind I crave, *is* a problem. It is wrong. "Bella," I say softly, and it is both a call to her to come to me and a plea for her to walk away.

She never gets the chance. My cellphone rings again. I grimace and reach for it, only to find Dash Black on the caller ID. "It's your brother," I say.

Her chest lifts with a heavy breath, her eyes meeting mine again, and the discomfort of the moment is palpable. She laughs a choked laugh. "Of course, it is. I'm not here," she says softly. "Okay?"

Because Dash wouldn't approve, now more than ever, I suspect. I know it. The fact that she knows it says to me they've had conversations about me. I know this, too, but I still don't like it. "As you wish, Bella," I reply, my voice soft, but there's nothing about anything I feel right now that is as gentle as my words.

I answer the call. "Dash," I greet tightly.

"Are you going to the memorial?" he asks, and I don't doubt his concern. He might not want me fucking around with his sister, but we do have a friendship I wouldn't call it tenuous as much as I would strained.

"My mother called it off."

He expels a sigh that reads like relief. "I can't believe she thought that was a good idea. You need company? I can head over."

Bella's eyes collide with mine, panic in their depths, an indicator to me that she can hear the conversation. "I'm better off alone tonight," I say tightly. "I know you get that. I know you know why that feels necessary."

I'm selling the moment to Dash, ensuring he stays away, but the words seem to punch at Bella, and she physically steps backward. She's read a message into the words only meant to drive Dash away. She rotates and disappears inside my apartment, and I find the idea of her leaving stirs an odd mix of resistance and relief in me. Her brother has now soundly inserted himself between us and he doesn't even know. He should be the one feeling relief, not me. He has the joy of sweet ignorance while I do not.

I'm ready to pursue Bella when Dash says, "You sure about that?"

I turn away from the apartment and face the city night. "I have my ways of coping, just like you do."

"That's what I'm afraid of," he says.

"I'm not a drunk, Dash," I bite out. "I'm an opportunist and often booze is easier to deal with than human beings."

"And I'm not a fight junkie. Come on, man. We both know you tip that bottle too easily. If you don't want to see me tonight, call one of your many women. Better to bury yourself in one of them than a bottle."

My lips pull tightly over my teeth. "I'll keep that in mind. Now if you're done coddling me—"

"All right, Tyler. I'll let you go, but you need family now. Bella comes over on Saturdays and makes waffles. Why don't you come tomorrow morning?"

"I am not the waffle and family kind of guy."

"Maybe you should be."

"Or not. Thanks for the check-in. Now goodbye." I disconnect and rotate back to the apartment.

I never heard the door. I don't think Bella left.

I walk inside the apartment, and I do so with Dash's advice on my mind. Better to bury myself in Bella than a bottle. Not his specific words, but close enough.

21

LISA RENEE JONES

CHAPTER FOUR

Tyler

It should really surprise no one that I have a dominant side and a need for control.

In light of that reality, by the time I've shut the sliding glass door, and sealed myself inside, I've already conjured an image of a submissive version of Bella at my command. Me on my couch, her naked and lying across my lap, with my palm on her backside. A safe fantasy, considering I have no intention of acting on it. Hand to cock is about the only relief in sight on this night because I have zero interest at this moment in anyone but Bella. But it's a hell of a fantasy I allow myself because it's better than all the other places my head has been the past two hours.

As if she knows I'm better off with her than without her, the object of my fantasy is indeed still here. Of course, she is, as I've thought before tonight, this is Bella. And Bella never runs from any challenge I offer her, even if that challenge is managing to visit my apartment and leave without ever ending up naked.

She's now curled up in the chair, a blanket covering her, an open pint, and a spoon in hand. I step to the end of the couch and stare down at her right as she shovels a giant spoonful into her mouth. "I thought about leaving, but the ice cream is perfectly soft right now, and it's really wet outside."

My brows shoot up, and her cheeks flush but her lips purse. "That only sounded bad because you have a dirty mind. Which is better than a sad one, I suppose,

23

though I generally think it's a male disease to turn everything into sex." She waves the spoon at me and then at the table. "Eat the soft ice cream. Believe it or not, some things are better soft."

If we're talking about her in my arms, she's right. I ease into the space of the sitting area and sit down. "What happened to the chocolate peanut butter?"

"You can try it, but you can't have it," she says, lifting the pint in her hand.

"What happened to this being my pity party?"

"Pity is for—" She bites her lips and stops herself.

I supply her answer. "Pussies?"

"Yeah, that," she says. "And you are many things, Tyler, but not that."

"Now I'm intrigued," I assure her. "What am I then, Bella?"

"Eat the ice cream and I'll consider my answer while you do."

I'm actually hungry, and while a steak would suit me better, I do like a good helping of ice cream. I pick up the cookie dough pint and pull off the lid."

"I knew you'd go for that one."

"Because you took my favorite option."

She sits up and lets the blanket fall away, leaning close to offer me access to her pint, which is better than no access at all. "You can taste, but that's all." She smiles, and I suspect she knows exactly what she's doing, but it's hard to read Bella. She comes off that damn sweet, when I know she is far from the naivete that sweetness suggests.

If only she meant I could taste her, and if she was anyone else, I'd do that and more. Instead, I dig my spoon into the ice cream and then taste it. She watches me, and I don't miss the parting of her perfect, plump lips as if she's anticipating my reaction. It's truly an

24

alternate reality. She should be anticipating where my mouth will go next on her body, not my reaction to ice cream.

I allow the milky sweet richness to melt in my mouth, and it's better than I expect. Not better than the taste of her, I am sure, but better than I expect. "It's good," I declare softly, my gaze falling to her mouth, and lingering as I contemplate how sweet she might be, how soft her moans.

When my eyes find hers again, the rain is splattering the floor-to-ceiling windows, the intimacy of the dimly lit room, of my stare and shared ice cream from the same container, thickens the air between us, and I have no doubt my gaze is pure lust.

She doesn't play the shy one and cut her stare. Bella is a contradiction of sweet and bold in ways that test my desire to see her submissive, but I'd be willing to teach her. "I was just teasing you about only having a taste," she dares. "You can have whatever you want."

There's an invitation in her words, be it intentional or not, but there are other words in my head, beating down my hunger for Bella. Allison's words. The words from the journal play in my head, *the heart wants what the heart wants.* I'd reason with myself that this is about what the body wants, which is an entirely different thing. But I cannot be so blasé about Bella, not when my guilt over Allison's death might as well be the actual ghost of Allison whispering in my ear— demanding that I be better and do better by Bella than I did with her.

"I don't think that would be fair of me, now, would it?" I ask, and I'm not talking about taking her ice cream. For all I know she really was, and I'm simply the bastard one would expect my father's son to become. I sit back and reach for the pint I've opened. "This one is good."

Considering my cock is hard as fuck and ice cream is the closest thing to a cold shower in my near future, I dig in. For long moments, that perhaps stretch into minutes, we eat in silence. In that silence I do not find awkwardness, nor do I find peace. I find accusation and blame. I find the screams of a woman who left this world too soon, and because of me. I cannot touch Bella. I will not touch Bella. If I had just left Allison alone, she might be alive today. And while I'm fairly certain Bella would be the death of me, not the opposite, it's not a risk I can take. Though it would be a punishment I deserve.

CHAPTER FIVE

"You didn't kill her, Tyler," Bella blurts as if she is reading my mind.

I glance over at her. "I did my part."

"Should you have gotten involved with an employee?" she asks, setting her pint down. "No. Does it happen? All the time and no one dies. You're human."

"And she's dead."

"Because she chose to get involved with your father. Because he chose to kill her. You were not a party to the decisions that lead to her death."

"I started the cycle."

"Did you? Because there are rumors that she dated him before you and then went back to him."

The idea punches me in the gut for reasons I can't even let myself identify right now. "That's not true."

"How do you know?"

I set the ice cream down, reach for the journal and lift it. "Because she wrote about it all. Because the police say so. Because *she* said so."

Bella curls her fingers around the blanket and eases back into the chair again. "How long has it been since you dated her?'

"Over a year."

"That's a long time, Tyler. Too long for you to wrap yourself in the blame game."

I set the journal on the table beside the ice cream, taunting us both with its presence. "If you read her words, you'd hate me."

"You try to make me hate you most days at work, and you still don't succeed. I'm not easily manipulated. Relationships always have two subjective sides, and I have no business inside yours. Neither did your father. He tried to demean your role at Hawk Legal every chance he got. He was getting old, and he wasn't ready to let you be the king of the castle. No doubt, he wanted what you have. Youth, success, and her. He did this, not you. Remember that. *Please.*"

I pick up the ice cream pint again, wondering how she'd react if I mixed a shot in with it.

She scoots forward and grabs the remote to the television. Instinctively, I set down the ice cream and reach out and grab her hand. She sucks in a breath. I hold one in, a muscle in my jaw pulsing. I've made the mistake of removing the contact barrier and now that I've touched her, I want to keep touching her.

Her eyes lift to mine, and she clears her throat. "If you don't want to watch TV—"

I force myself to let her go, not pull her to me, dropping her hand before I lose the resolve to do so. "I don't want to watch the news. The media can't seem to talk about anything but my family."

"I was thinking about torturing you with a chick flick. I saw on my listings earlier that Dirty Dancing is showing. Patrick Swayze." She sighs and thumps her chest with her fist. "Be still my heart." She indicates the remote. "Can I?"

"I've never watched a chick flick in my life. Somehow today doesn't seem like that day."

Her eyes go wide. "Never?"

"Never."

She does this delicate little grunt thing and says, "Just one of the many reasons you're single at thirty-four."

That comment shouldn't jab as badly as it does, but mixed with Allison's words in the journal, it downright stings. "By choice," I assure her, and considering I'm more than a little curious about her love life, I add, "And you're single as well."

"By choice," she assures me, offering me not even a tease about her personal life. "And I'm twenty-seven, not thirty-four." She gives me this little chin tilt, as if it celebrates the perfection of her comeback reply, then adds, "I really thought something warmhearted rather than murderous was a good idea right about now."

She's not wrong. I motion to the remote. "Turn on your damn chick flick."

She smiles, and it lights up the room, and I swear even a tiny spot in my black heart, right along with it. She turns on the television, and before the news can begin to play, punches in the station of choice. Patrick Swayze fills the screen. I finish off my ice cream, every last bite, and Bella does the same. I gather two additional pints and carry them to the fridge. When I return, her eyes are shut. I sit back down and find myself staring at her. Just staring at her, spellbound by her beauty, which is more than her looks, which are obviously stunning. Bella's beauty radiates from within.

Thunder claps like heavy hands above and while I jolt with the impact, she does not. She feels safe here with me, and I can't figure out why. But then, maybe she knows more about me than me, because when I should be stripping her naked and pulling her onto my lap, I am not. Just as I should wake her up and send her on her way.

But I don't.

The truth, which I would never admit to anyone, is I don't want to be alone.

I ease into the couch cushion, low and comfortable, and shut my eyes.

When I open them again, the room is dark, the rain has faded into the night. I blink and sit up, to realize the movie has long ended and *Terminator* is playing. Clearly, this channel plays old movies. My eyes land on the chair where Bella rested, only to find the blanket on the ground and her missing. The idea that she left while I slept is oddly anger-inducing. Why the fuck did she leave? And why the fuck am I unhappy about it?

I stand, my spine stiff, and that's when I see her shoes on the floor. She's still here. Where the hell is she? A sound reaches my ears from my bedroom, and my anger ratchets up tenfold. Why is she in my bedroom? What game is she playing? I step around the couch and walk toward the fireplace and enter my room just to the right of the crackling flame.

The room smells of her perfume and my cock twitches.

The bathroom door is shut and holy hell I'm hot and hard at the idea that she's naked in there, and planning to surprise me. But I'm still as angry as I am burning alive at the prospect. I can't protect her from me when I'm battling with what it even means to be me. I'm not in the right headspace for games of the flesh when they pertain to Bella.

I step to the door and knock, the thundering of my fist on the wood no match for the pounding in my chest or the throb of my cock. The door swings open and Bella appears, still fully dressed. The mix of disappointment and relief is not pleasant and does nothing to eliminate my anger, but rather these things spike it times ten.

"What are you doing in my bedroom?" I demand.

Her eyes go wide, a blush rushing over her otherwise pale skin, creating a blood-red stain. I don't miss the way it blanches her neck and rapidly travels toward her neckline. Nor do I stop myself from wondering just how far down it reaches.

"I ah—" she murmurs. "I couldn't figure out where the guest bathroom was. I had to go badly and—I'm sorry."

It's as reasonable as it is unreasonable, considering the bathroom is right beside the door. "Coming here was not a smart decision. You need to leave."

"You're being a jerk."

"Yes, well, you can choose if you hate me before or after your legs are wrapped around my neck, Bella. Because that's what's going to happen if you don't leave now." I step backward and give her room to exit.

Her spine straightens and her chin lifts in defiance. "We're friends."

"Friends don't fuck and that's exactly where my head is right now. I told you. You have two options—"

"I heard you," she snaps. "I don't need to hear it again. I'll leave. You're being a bastard."

"Because I am a bastard, Bella. You've been warned. I won't warn you again."

She steps out of the bathroom and stops in front of me. "I said you're being a bastard, not that you *are* one. It's too bad you don't understand the difference." With that, she marches out of the room, and without turning, I know when she exits the bedroom. I feel the shift in the air.

I stand there, I don't follow her, or I won't let her leave.

There's shuffling about and then the door opens. The door shuts.

Then I'm alone again. And that's the way it should be. She might hate me, but she left here before she did something she might regret, even if I would not.

CHAPTER SIX

Tyler

Two months later...

When a butterfly spreads her wings, you never clip them. You admire them from afar. Bella is a butterfly. A beautiful, blonde butterfly with gorgeous blue eyes, and a fiery personality that spans a rainbow of colors. Not to mention intelligence, negotiation skills, and a body that would rock any man's world. Especially in the black, form-fitting dress, she's wearing tonight. I watch her from the other side of Hawk Legal's rooftop entertainment area as she mingles with a mix of the rich and famous clients we cater to here at the firm.

With a full two months passing since his death, we still battle the whispers in the hallways and among our clients about my father, the killer, the monster. The disgrace.

Tonight should have been the ringing in of a new era, with me officially the reigning CEO, and President of the Hawk empire. But outside of the complexity of our business, which stretches far beyond legal services, is the complexity of my father withholding his will for sixty days. The final details of which should have concluded yesterday. That was until the attorney, and executor of the will, went off and broke his arm skiing in Colorado. Now it will be days longer before the details of my inheritance and the company handoff are revealed.

Bella does a little twirl, obviously, a part of a story she's telling, and the faces around her light up, the clients she's entertaining are obviously charmed and quite properly.

Allison wasn't a butterfly or she'd never have sought out my father after I turned her away from my bed. She was a firefly lighting up the night, always a spark to be found, and most of it in the form of attitude. The two women could not have been more unalike.

Bella laughs, and while I can't hear the sweet sound of her voice, her head tilts back, the creamy expanse of her neck on display, and my damn cock twitches. It twitches every damn time she walks into my office, the ice queen who has frozen me out since I showed her the bastard in me is alive and well.

I think about how close I came to taking her to my bed, how close I came to fucking her until she saw stars. But she is not for me, I remind myself—*yet again.* It would break me, but that is a joke, *I* would break *her.* She would hate me. She came to my apartment to keep me company and I needed that company. Translation: she's too damn good of a friend and a person for my hand to burn her the way it abso-fucking-lutely would if I got the chance again to make it happen.

Because I wouldn't let things end as they did last time if there was a next time between us.

I turn away from the glorious sight of her and rest my hands on the railing overlooking the bright lights of Nashville's bustling downtown. The February night is unseasonably warm enough to open the balcony doors but there is a chill in the air, the knowledge that my father left this world a man without honor. I vow right here and now that I will never allow myself to become a monster like Jack Hawk.

"Hey."

At the sound of Bella's voice, a punch of unruly awareness burns through my veins. There is something about this woman. There has *always* been *something* about Bella. *She is off limits*, I tell myself before I even consider acknowledging her. I did the wrong things, even if I felt like they were right at the time. I rotate to face her, each of us resting an arm on the railing.

"Bella," I greet.

She searches my face, far too comfortable in her intimate inspection when no one else finds me this approachable. But then, she is Bella. That is the answer I have to all things with this woman. No one else would have come to me after my father died, fed me ice cream, and then forced Patrick Swayze doing *Dirty Dancing* on me. Despite her track record of boldly going where no one else will go with me, she has also kept her distance these past two months. This is why I am shocked when she lifts her hand to touch my hand and briefly touches my arm before she awkwardly pulls back.

She has never touched me outside of that night at my apartment, and even then, the collision of our hands reaching for the remote had been accidental. I'd wanted to fuck her. She would have let me, too. I'd seen it in her eyes, felt it in the air between us, a warm blanket of lust and desire cloaking us in the moment. But she would have regretted it the next day.

But that memory lingers with me, and in her touch just now, it's ignited. She is standing close enough that I can smell the jasmine sweet perfume she wears tonight as she had that night, and I'm hot and hard, the zipper to my expensive blue suit stretched and ready to break. No doubt a product of the fantasy in my head right now, involving her naked and in my arms while my cock is buried inside her. She'd beg me for more. I'd give it to her, too.

She must read my reaction, the primal need to drag her away and fuck her kind of feeling, because she whispers, "Tyler?"

"Yes, Bella?"

"You okay?" she asks.

I have no idea why she believes I would be anything but fine and then some. It's in this moment that I think that maybe, just maybe, I should just fuck this woman out of my system and me out of hers. I don't want a friendship that involves sympathy and an assumption that I am weak when I am not. "I'm just fine. Are you?"

She wets her lips nervously, her delicate little pink tongue stroking over skin when it really should be my tongue all over her body. She gives a short laugh. "I'm fine. Why wouldn't I be?"

"You tell me," I urge softly, baiting her when I should be reassuring her.

It's a game I'm playing with her, one I cannot resist despite good reason. Because it's a dangerous game. For her, not me.

CHAPTER SEVEN

Tyler

The exchange between myself and Bella lingers in the air...

Her: *You okay?*

Me: *I'm just fine. Are you?*

There's a flicker of something in Bella's eyes that I cannot name with that rebuttal question I've handed her one moment and dashed away the next with what appears to be sheer determination. My gut feeling is that whatever she wants to say to me has been set aside. As if proving my assumption, she dismisses the question and in a typical Bella move, does exactly what I did to her. She turns the topic back to me. "This isn't about me tonight. It's about you," she declares. "It's a big deal to take over the family empire. But I want you to know that everyone here tonight, and everyone I've communicated with since your father's death, seems relieved to have you officially steering the ship's wheel."

"Even Dash?" I ask because I believe that is who she is talking about, reassuring me that I'm right with her brother, who was more than a little put off by me only months before. I'd not only pulled him from an underground fight, but I'd also used Bella and the woman he's now marrying to help me with the process. He'd been embarrassed, but he'd kept his film deal, and his woman.

"Dash knows you were there for him."

"He didn't at the time."

"No," she confirms, "but that was then, and this is now. He's reached out to you for a reason. He's officially over his anger. Just as you're officially the captain of this ship."

The reference to my position being "official" punches me in the gut, but I manage not to flinch despite the voice of concern nagging at my mind, telling me my father hated me. He will never make my takeover easy, no matter how inevitable it is. I skip this reality check with Bella. It's Thursday night. My concerns will no longer be concerns at all come Monday morning. "And I'm not polarizing?" I challenge, interested in how she dodges this bullet, not how I dodge my own.

"I'd label you as demanding and arrogant," she replies with no hesitation in her answer. "You can also be sharp and intolerant."

I narrow my eyes on her. "You know no one else talks to me like that, right?"

"You asked, and if I'm the only person you believe will really answer, then the staff must not know that you value honesty and directness. You really should fix that."

"Should I now?"

"Yes, you should."

"And how do *you* know I value honestly and directness?"

"Because that's how you operate, no matter how uncomfortable honesty and directness might make everyone around you."

My lips curve. "Are you talking about the night you came to my apartment?"

Her cheeks turn pink and there is a bristle to the air. That something in her eyes is back but, in a blink, she erases her emotions. "Or perhaps the time you told me that being a woman could be an advantage or disadvantage and I had to choose which. In that situation, you said I was being a scared little girl when I let a Hollywood studio walk on me. I wasn't offended. You were not gentle, but gentle is not what I needed."

She has no idea how much I want to prove those words right.

She continues with, "You *can be* a bastard when you so *choose to be*, Tyler. But you are not *a bastard*. Those are two different things. Just as one can be bad, but not be a bad person."

My eyes narrow and I ask, "Am I *bad*, Bella?"

"It depends on how you define bad," she replies.

"How do *you* define bad?"

"Privately," she replies shortly. "And based on my previous reprimand, I'll keep that to myself, but I've been keeping way too much to myself now."

"Ah," I reply. "Now it seems we're going to get to the real reason you found me in the crowd."

Her spine stiffens slightly, and her eyes meet mine. "I need to talk business with you tomorrow and I don't like that I should have done so three days ago and did not. I hesitated."

I arch a brow. "Why, exactly, did you hesitate?"

"Perhaps expectations got the best of me," she replies in a statement colored with hidden meaning. "But now my own desire for perfection wins. We need to talk this out."

In other words, she was forced to tear down the wall between us despite every effort to leave it firmly in place. "If the topic you wish to speak to me about is three days old, talk now."

"It's a long debate on some of the final film negotiations for Dash's Hollywood contract. A topic worthy of time and privacy, and while I doubt either of us appreciates those things right now, both are necessary."

"I have always opened my door for you when you needed me."

"Just not when *you* need *me*, right?" she challenges softly, and the heat of her cheeks tells me the words have slipped out. "Forget I said that."

My eyes narrow on her and I say, "Me wanting the time and privacy with you was never the question, Bella. I told you—"

"I remember exactly what you told me quite vividly." Her tone is unquestionably tart.

Which tells me that she's thinking about me suggesting her legs would end up around my neck. "Bella—"

She cuts me off, "I'll buzz your secretary when I get in tomorrow and get on your schedule." She starts to turn.

That intolerance she credited me for is alive and well, as I say, "Bella," my tone crisp and authoritative. It's a command that she not walk away from me.

She halts and hesitates a beat before she complies with my wishes and turns to face me. I close the two steps she's placed between us and say, "I made you leave because—"

"You're a bastard?" she challenges.

"I am a bastard, Bella. You wanted to be my friend. *I wanted* your legs around my neck. I wanted my mouth all over your body. I wanted my tongue in the most intimate part of your body. Don't push me, or that's where we'll end up and that's not good for either of us." I catch her elbow with my hand and the charge I expect darts between us, a message in and of itself. My hand falls from her arm, and I say, "Don't walk away. Run away. Understand?"

Her eyes lower and then lift. "Yes, sir," she replies softly, but she doesn't cut her stare, nor does she *ever* call me sir. It's almost as if she's intentionally showing me a submissive side meant to tempt me into testing her. If she was anyone else, I'd think it was an invitation.

But Bella would never bow down, not even in play. This is no invitation. It's punishment.

And while my sins might come in many different forms in her mind, in my mind, it's pushing her away, instead of fucking her.

LISA RENEE JONES

CHAPTER EIGHT

Bella

I can feel Tyler's eyes on me and if that wasn't enough to undo me, the impact of his touch—that small touch on my elbow—lingers, and in places he didn't touch. Or lick. I just cannot believe he said what he said or how affected by his words and the man, in general, I truly am, at least in a public place. My breasts are heavy, my nipples tight. My thighs are slick.

I've known this man for years.

How did we get here now?

But somehow, I continue to work the room, interacting with clients until it's reasonable for me to claim a breather. I step outside, onto a quiet portion of the outdoor area framing the lounge area. My hands catch the edge of the wall and I draw in a breath, the cool air offering sweet relief to my warm skin. Seconds tick by and the burn in my belly begins to ease, allowing my mind the opportunity to hunt for reason in feelings.

When I was sixteen, my father's star status as a NASCAR driver was ever so present in my life and so was the social side of that scene. At that time, I knew all about boys, boys, and more boys, and yes, men. There was a man, a driver on my father's team, who made my stomach flutter and my knees weak. That same driver is now a competitor with his own car, who has hit on me too many times to count and he's gotten nowhere. Because he only wants me to hurt my father.

In other words, I've known a few bastards.

Maybe Tyler is one of them, maybe he is not.

I didn't know the driver—David is his name—was a bastard when I was being attacked by butterflies. And in the years I've worked with Tyler, I've been a mix of what I might call butterflies and bees. I've never known a man that I can alternatively hate and lust for, until this one. And he's my boss. He was right to send me away that night at his apartment. And I'm better off hating him.

"Bella."

The male voice that greets me does not belong to Tyler, and I hate the disappointment this realization creates in me. I should be pleased. Distance between me and Tyler is not only appropriate, it's safe. I rotate to greet Josh Henry, the business manager for a rather large country singer, who is not only writing a book, he's entering Hollywood with my help. Since I've managed most of my brother's Hollywood endeavors, I've somehow become the company Hollywood "it" girl where agenting comes into play.

"I didn't know you were here," I greet him, my way of letting him know I haven't intentionally avoided him, even if at times that would be my preference. Josh is a handsome man who personifies tall, dark, and good-looking. The kind of man who wears a suit like the cover of GQ magazine, but still not as well as Tyler. Josh is a woman magnet—a fact he embraces a bit too well. He takes liberties he believes this earns him. In other words, he can get as handsy as he does cocky.

"Is Malcolm here?" I ask of his client, hoping for the buffer between Josh and me Malcolm always proves himself.

"It's his mother's sixtieth birthday this weekend. He took her to Paris."

"That's amazing of him," I say, and even now, as a grown adult, there are times when I hear something like this, and I feel a twist in my heart at the loss of my own mother despite that being a lifetime ago. Since I was a kid, actually. "He's a good guy in a swarm of bad ones," I add, reminded of the whole "*am I bad?*" exchange with Tyler.

Josh steps to the railing beside me and I rotate to face him again. He's close, too close to be professional, but the barriers of decorum are rarely barriers to him at all. "You look beautiful tonight, Bella," he says, his voice warm when it should not be.

I laugh off the compliment. "Thank you, but you say that every time you see me."

"And you say that every time you see me. Take the compliment, Bella. It's deserved."

"So is Malcolm's success. How are you feeling about Tyler taking over Hawk Legal?"

"Sympathetic to the mess he has to clean up, but if you're asking if I'm concerned about his ability to manage it, no. Jack was never the person anyone believed was running the show, no matter how much he wanted us to believe otherwise."

"So you came to show Tyler support," I assume.

His eyes light with mischief. "And you. We've got big things ahead this year. Why don't we go to have a drink and celebrate?"

And here we go, I think. "I thought that's what we were doing here tonight?"

"Alone," he says, and then his hand is on my waist, his head dipping low, near my face. "You have no idea the fantasies I have about my hands on your body."

I reach for his solidly placed hand and try to push it away. "This is not okay, Josh. Please remove your hand."

"You heard the lady. Remove your hand or I will."

I gasp and look up to find Tyler standing beside us, tightly controlled but obvious anger burning in the stare he's focused on Josh.

CHAPTER NINE

Bella

"If you'd like my hands on you," Tyler replies, when Josh has yet to move away from me, "I'll have no problem with making a scene."

Josh's hand falls from my waist and he places space between me and him. And it seems, Tyler, who is now standing beside me, faces Josh. "What is between me and Bella is not your business, Tyler."

I bristle. "There's nothing but business between us, Josh."

Tyler replies with a laser focus on Josh, "Bella is my business. It would be a mistake to assume otherwise."

There is something wholly possessive about the way Tyler says those words, but I tell myself this is about my job and my role as his employee, rather than me, myself, and my womanhood. However, all of this feels quite personal with both men.

"I think it's best if you leave, Josh," Tyler adds tightly.

Josh dares to step closer to us again, to Tyler specifically. "Malcolm won't like the way you're talking to me."

"Malcolm is a valued client and a friend," Tyler rebuts. "If you don't know we grew up next door to each other, or that he was one of the first people to call me when my father died, you don't know your client well. If anyone parts ways with Malcolm over this, it's you. He won't like what I have to say about it. And he knows Bella opened doors for him, others will not."

"We'll see about that," Josh replies, and he steps around Tyler and starts walking.

Automatically, Tyler and I rotate to watch him weave through the crowd. When he disappears from sight, Tyler pursues him. My heart leaps with concern, and I'm instantly on his heels, still there as he exits the room and steps into the hallway. I catch the door that would shut in my face and find only Tyler in the hallway. The elevator banks are empty, which indicates to me that either Josh got lucky, and the doors were open, allowing his quick escape, or he took the stairs. He was running from Tyler while I am not, despite him commanding me to do just that.

The door shuts behind me and Tyler turns to face me. "My office, Ms. Bailey," he states flatly.

"*Ms. Bailey?*" I challenge, with this new formality between us.

That's all he says before he strides toward the elevators and punches the button. I'd think I was about to be fired if he hadn't just assured Josh I'd be working with Malcolm, just not him. The elevator doors open and Tyler glances over at me. "Are you coming?"

He told me to run away and now he's inviting me into a tiny little car, alone with him. It's not as if I've never been in an elevator with him before this, but it's never felt quite as intimidating. But then, I've never allowed myself to crumble beneath a veil of intimidation and I won't start now. I march toward Tyler and since he's holding the door, I pass him and step inside the car. I don't make eye contact. I'll save that part of my grandstanding for after we're in the little bitty box that moves up and down and allows no escape while doing so.

Tyler joins me and punches in the office floor, which is on a lower level, the earthy, masculine scent of man and cologne recreating those damn butterflies in my belly. We stand there, side by side, staring forward, and watch the doors shut. The tension between us crackles and while I intend to say nothing, that never really works out for me.

I rotate to face him. "Shouldn't we be downstairs attending to our clients?"

He steps around and faces me. "We've both made ourselves available for hours. The staff will wrap up the night. We are done."

"Are we going to lose Malcolm as a client?"

The elevator halts and dings before he says, "Mark my words that it would be a bad decision for Malcolm to leave us when his manager had his hands all over you." The doors open and he motions for me to exit.

He's angry and I'm not sure I've ever actually seen Tyler angry. For a moment, my feet plant with my resistance to our little meeting in his office but whatever this is, wherever it leads, it's inevitable that we see it through. And not in an elevator with cameras.

I force my feet from the ground and exit the car. To the right are the main offices. To the left, are Tyler's private offices, which are locked up behind glass doors. I pause, waiting on Tyler, and he moves ahead of me. With unexplainable weak knees, I walk with him and then wait as he unlocks the door, which he holds open for me to enter the lobby first.

Tyler watches me with veiled lids, and I feel his attention with a rush of heat over my skin, which is enough to tell me everything about me and Tyler feels different. And I react outwardly as well, and no doubt, he notices my quick inhalation of breath, the tell-all sign that I'm nervous for no good reason. I've had confrontations with Tyler. I've been to his office and even been there when it was only the two of us. And yet today, as I walk past him and enter the lobby when I would normally charge ahead to prove I'm in charge of this battle, I do nothing of the sort.

Instead, I wait for him, and he arches a brow, motioning me forward. I meet his stare, the spark between us undeniable and I say, "Your office. You first."

His lips quirk slightly, and I think he's amused. I am not. "As you wish, Ms. Bailey."

"Stop calling me that," I chide. "Bella. I've always been Bella."

The quirk widens and he neither agrees nor disagrees with my demand, but he does move forward, walking ahead of me. I fall into step behind him and try not to notice his ass in his perfectly fitted suit. I'm not supposed to look at my boss' ass, but by keeping my eyes level, I instead notice his broad shoulders and tall frame. Six-foot-three I've heard whispered in the hallways because the females in the firm do whisper about Tyler Hawk.

Just not me.

And yet, my body is whispering plenty.

I have this sense that I am about to be caged with a primal animal, but that is more about my reaction to his words than his actions.

The truth is, I am going to be alone with Tyler, and I can't stop thinking about his reference to his tongue on my body.

CHAPTER TEN

Bella

I follow Tyler down the hallway toward his office, nerves settling in my belly in a tight little ball. The stiffness of his spine oozes arrogance, but there is an edge to him that I believe to be confirmation of his anger. This realization is a reality check. This would be a good time to get my head out of the bedroom.

This is business, not personal, and I have my job to think about. What happened upstairs with Josh was inappropriate and therefore serious business. Scandal has landed on the steps of Hawk Legal and Tyler carries that load. What if he actually believes Josh hit on me because everyone but him knows that I've slept my way to success? The mere idea of such a thing is both appalling and embarrassing, as well as untrue. But the memory of me visiting Tyler's house and using his master bathroom—I truly saw no other bathroom— does not sit well in my defense, no matter how innocent my intentions were.

I went there that night, worried about him, and now I question where my head was when I made that decision. *Thinking about losing my mother*, I remind myself. I'd just come off the holidays and it was near the anniversary of her death and I just—well, I wasn't thinking at all. I mean, I know Tyler Hawk isn't exactly the kind of man who operates with emotion. I just also know things about him from Dash that perhaps I should not know.

The hallway ends and the fact that Tyler enters his office before me rather than waiting on me sets the tone. He has now transitioned to boss mode instead of whatever else was happening between us, and that's a comfortable place for me to operate. I know him in boss mode. I know myself in employee mode, albeit one willing to challenge him when, as he said, not many others will. Nevertheless, this is a space we have operated in for years now. I can do this.

Mental pep talk aside, I follow Tyler into his office and I'm in fight mode, determined to defend myself, expecting to find him behind his desk. He is not. He's this side of his visitors' chairs, with no indication he plans to move. "Shut the door," he orders.

As if anyone else is here, I think, but the butterflies in my belly defy my newfound business state of mind. I'm not sure if I'm afraid for my job, or afraid of myself. Nevertheless, I shut the door and lean on the hard surface. "You don't approve of how I handled Josh." It's a statement, not a question.

"I don't see that you handled him at all," he replies dryly.

"I was in the process of removing his hand," I rebut, and it's the truth. I was in *the process*.

"Is that the first time he's hit on you?" he demands, obviously unmoved by my proclamation of impending action.

Damn it, I think, before admitting, "No, but—"

He steps closer, towering over me with his six-foot-three-inch height, no doubt meant to intimidate. "If you'd handled him," he states, his words chock full of derision, "he wouldn't repeat his mistake."

My feathers are officially ruffled, okay they're long past ruffled, but they're standing on end, at this point.

"That really worked with you." My sarcasm is oh, so intentional.

"I didn't touch you," he counters. "He did."

"And you think what you said to me was appropriate?" I challenge.

"As we've discussed," he replies, "I value honesty. I assume you do as well. You deserved to know the slippery slope you were walking on."

"You said—*things*—twice."

"Once before you touched me. A second time seemed like an appropriate warning when you touched me, Bella."

"I'm a touchy-feely person. It's part of how I communicate."

"And yet, you've never touched me until this past week. And as for how you communicate, what exactly *were* you trying to say to me, *Bella*?" His voice is low and raspy, and my nerve endings go nuts.

I slide right past the change in me where he's concerned, and there has been one. He's not wrong. For now, though, I focus on the truth I understand. "I was trying to tell you, that I'm an employee and a friend."

"*Friend*?" he challenges. "I wonder what that means to Josh? I think your communication skills need work."

Screw my ruffled feathers. Now I'm angry, too. "You know what?" I snap. "You barged into that situation like a protective bear. I've never *ever* let sex be a part of my job."

"Of course, you have. You know you get a little more time here or there because you're a beautiful woman."

My heart thunders in my chest. He thinks I'm *beautiful*? And of all things, right now, why is that what I just focused on?

"And I *am* protective of you, Bella," he adds, his attention sharply fixated on my face, but his stare is carefully veiled.

I am not moved by his words. I'm actually slightly offended. "Because I'm Dash's sister," I state, and it's not a question. I love my brother, but the weird, almost confrontational friendship between him and Dash, and I'm always in the middle.

"No," he says without hesitation. "I hired you before Dash was even part of the picture. Dash has nothing to do with anything between us."

I could read into the "*between us*" comment in an intimate way, and if I were someone else, I might. But I don't. I came to Nashville on my own, for a job. Dash followed me, not the other way around. My chin lifts in defiance. "Make no mistake. I can handle myself, Tyler."

He steps closer, and I can feel the heat of his body, the scent of his cologne, drugging my senses. "Show me," he challenges. "Handle *me* now."

A summersault of energy overwhelms me, my stomach feeling every second of the wicked twist that follows. "What does that even mean?"

He shocks me then, his hands sliding to my waist, a rush of heat between us, fire in my belly. "Handle me now," he repeats.

It is the first and only time Tyler Hawk has ever touched me, rather than me touching him, and I feel the connection in every part of me. I don't know what his intent is right now, or what he wants from me, but I know we're treading on dangerous ground.

And I'm the one who will get hurt.

I should run away from him as he suggested.

But I am going nowhere.

CHAPTER ELEVEN

Bella

My hand goes to Tyler's hand, which rests on my waist, in my mind trying to control what comes next but all it does is create another connection, me to him and him to me. But he's also simply imitating what Josh did to me out on that patio—where he touched me, how he touched me. But there is no comparison. One is ice and one is heat. Tyler is the heat. "You are not Josh."

"Why does that matter?" he challenges. "This is an exercise in control. Your control, Bella."

My eyes meet his and I swear, I have that same sensation I had when he first touched me. I feel him in every part of me. "What are you doing, Tyler?" I whisper. "What are *we* doing?"

"Tell me no, Bella," he demands, his voice low but no less commanding.

"No," I say easily, but it's not exactly the version of "no" he's asking for. I'm not saying "no" to his touch. I'm saying "no" to saying "no" to Tyler. Because I can't seem to will myself any more than him to remove his hand from my body.

Tyler rather obviously senses the real meaning behind my version of "no."

I see that in the way he narrows his eyes on me and I feel it in the flex of his fingers on my waist. There is possessiveness in the warmth of his touch that I might be imagining, but I am so screwed because I really hope that I am not. As if confirming my suspicions, he says, "Define your version of no, Bella."

I push back, rebelling against the command I've read in his tone. "I said what you wanted me to say."

His other hand comes down on the door beside my head, almost as if he's caging me. "Tell me no, Bella." There is something almost raw and angry in his words.

"Tyler—"

He shocks me then, cupping my face, his grip firm but not painful. "Is this how you tell everyone else no, Bella? Because if it is—"

"Don't be an asshole," I snap back at him. "I told you, you are not everyone else. And if you think I sleep around to get business, stop touching me and fire me, Tyler. I will happily pack up my desk today."

Seconds tick by in which he stares down at me, his blue eyes piercing, the air thick between us until he abruptly twines his fingers into my hair, giving the long strands a rough, erotic tug. His mouth lowers, lingering above mine, his breath on my skin. "I do not think you sleep around but damn it, woman, you *really* don't take orders well. I said, *say no,* and then this ends right now."

"I already did. You didn't like my version of 'no.'"

The muscle in his jaw flexes, seconds ticking by before he murmurs, "If there is one thing I've learned that you need to understand, it's that there are consequences to actions. This is what happens when you don't say no." His mouth closes down on my mouth, and then he's kissing me.

The world spins around me with the shock of the moment, and there is no thinking on my part to be found. I know he shouldn't be kissing me. I know I shouldn't kiss him back, but I do. I know I should stop this right here and now. *No* is the right response, he is right on that point. Because he is my boss, and the repercussions of our actions do have consequences. But the truth is, I just cannot seem to care. I don't even try. Though my hands don't move—one remains pressed to his where it rests on my waist, the other on his chest though I don't remember how it got there—I moan for him. I sink into the kiss, drinking in every moment of the sinful play of his mouth against my mouth.

When his lips part mine, I burn for more. I want to pull his mouth back to mine, but he lingers a breath from another kiss, so close, but out of reach. Time stands still, expanding over eternity it seems, and yet in an illogical contrast, too quickly. I am barely hanging onto my sanity, as the beats drum by.

Beats that could morph into regret and worry, if I'm allowed to think too much longer about facing the consequences of my actions tomorrow. Or even hours from now. I could almost convince myself he was going to find the good sense I do not apparently possess, and end this, after what was some lesson to me on why no is no. But that's not what happens.

He leans in and brushes his lips over mine, a gentle touch contrasted by his teeth catching my bottom lip roughly, a promise of something dark and delicious in that act. But I've always known Tyler has a darker side to him. I breathe out with the sensation spiraling through me, and he reaches up and drags the zipper down the front of my dress until it ends just above my belly button. His eyes, emotionless but for the hunger in their depths, meet mine, a challenge in their depths. I don't know if he wants me to say no now or if he's daring me to keep going.

He all but ensures I ride this out, pressing the lace cups of my bra down, exposing my ample breasts and nipples. His gaze lowers, and he runs his tongue over his lips as if his mouth waters at the sight of me. I suck in air as he catches the puckered peaks of my nipples in his fingers. What follows is a rough tug and twist that both hurts and feels so good, so much so, that my knees turn wobbly. My sex clenches, and I'm slick between my thighs all over again, as I haven't been for a man in a very long time.

Maybe not ever.

It's the forbidden thing I assume, the reason I'm reacting to Tyler with such intensity. This is going nowhere good but the moment, and it has to end. I have to say no.

CHAPTER TWELVE

Bella

I don't say no.

In fact, I seem to have lost the ability to even define the meaning of the word no.

Tyler leans in and suckles my nipple, and there's a spasm in my sex, a tease of an orgasm not quite there. I've never felt such a thing from nothing more than a man's mouth on my nipples, but I have been hyperaware of Tyler for a lifetime, it seems. More so lately, for reasons, I don't even understand. At some point, something shifted between us, and it's how we ended up here. Wherever here is.

He abandons my nipples and I want to cry out in objection, even as he buries his face in my neck and drags the skirt of my dress up and over my hips. The rasp of his day-long stubble scrapes my neck, sending shivers down my spine, and he murmurs, "Where do you want my mouth now, Bella?"

I think he's just talking, I really do, but then he's pulling back, cupping my face, and staring down at me, even as he slides my panties aside. "Here?" he asks, gliding a finger along the slick line of my sex. "Because you're so wet for me, I know you want me here." His fingers just barely enter me, a tease that drives me wild. And leaves me desperate.

God, I don't want him to know *how* desperate.

My lashes lower and he squeezes my jaw. "Look at me."

My eyes pop open, and he rewards me by sliding his fingers inside. I pant and bite my lip. "Where do you want my mouth, Bella?" he demands again.

"Everywhere," I manage.

Demand lights his eyes. "I require more specific instructions."

I laugh without humor because nothing is funny with his fingers inside me all but assuring his mouth will soon travel just as intimate a path. His hand closes around my panties and he yanks them away without warning. I gasp and my fingers dig into his upper arms. "Tyler," I whisper.

Now he catches my upper arms, the only touch between us, when he asks, "Do you want me to lick your pussy, Bella?"

I can feel the rush of heat to my cheeks. "Can you just stop talking, please?"

"Please is a good word," he says. "But not the word I want right now. Say it. *Tyler, I want you to lick my pussy.*"

"No," I say, appalled, and the minute I say the word and with force, I know it's a mistake.

"Now you understand how to use that word." His hands fall away from me, and he steps backward.

My heart thunders in my chest and I grab the lapels of his suit, halting his departure, my naked breasts between us. "No, I don't want to say it. Yes, I want..." I wet my lips.

He arches a brow. "You want what?"

"Why must I say it?" I plead.

"Why can't you say it?" he counters, and his hands settle on my hips, his body crowding mine, his powerful legs framing mine as he presses me back against the door.

I know the answer to his question, of course. Those words he wants me to speak feel dirty and awkward, unnatural to me, though I also admit that on some level he's offering me a naughty escape from the good girl me. But he is also not a stranger, and a stranger who I could play naughty with and then disappear would be empowering. Instead, he is *my boss,* who I will see tomorrow morning if I even still have a job. Maybe I'm fooling myself into thinking I'm not proving to him I will use sex to get what I want.

Only all I really want is him, and at present, his mouth.

He lowers himself to his knees and leans in and licks my clit. I gasp all over again, sensations twisting and turning inside me. His eyes lift to mine. "Say it, baby," he says softly and there is the tiniest hint of tenderness in his voice, a reminder that we are more than this moment. "It's just you and me and it goes nowhere else. *Say it* and I promise you one hell of an orgasm."

I can feel myself soften like his words, and ease into the idea of being a bit more daring than I know myself to be, though, in contrast, my fingers curl into my palms. "I want..." I pant out a breath and rush through the entire sentence before I can stop myself, "I want you to lick my pussy."

His lips curve, his eyes burning with satisfaction, but there is no shame or embarrassment in me to follow. He doesn't give me time for such unimportant things. He licks my clit, twirling it, and then he's gently suckling me. And then his mouth comes down over me.

"Oh," I whisper, giving myself to the sensation of this intimacy, letting my head fall back against the wall.

And then he is licking me in what I can only call a merciless exploration, creating an overload of sensations. The flicking of his thumb on my clit, his tongue sliding left and right, and all over me. His big fingers pressing inside me, stretching me. I can hear the rasp of my heavy breathing, but I have no will to calm any of my reactions to what I feel, what he is making me feel.

My own fingers uncurl from my palm and one hand finds his shoulder, the other his head, but doesn't stay there long. He lifts my leg, pulling it over his shoulder, and the act presses me onto the door again. The position steals all control from me, locked into position, at the mercy of his tongue and fingers, as they stroke me, driving me wild. Blood roars in my ears and I am lost to all of the wicked things he is doing to me. No, I'm done in by it all. My sex clenches with an intense spasm and from there I tumble into the sweet bliss of release. Remotely, I can hear my own moans and my panting, but I'm beyond holding back anything from Tyler. I quake and quake some more until I collapse into a sated pile of nothing but bones and skin.

I barely register the moment Tyler sets my leg on the ground, nor the moment he stands up. He cups my face and reality zips right back into place. His mouth slants over my mouth, the sweet and yet salty taste of me flavoring my tongue. When I am certain there is more to come, he pulls back and asks, "Can you taste me on your lips, baby?"

I draw a breath because something has shifted in him—his energy and his tone reading darker.

He pulls my bra up and zips my dress before he slides my skirt down. "That's proof you don't know how to say no." He steps away from me and walks behind his desk while I stand there shell-shocked. Was this a game to him? A lesson like I'm a schoolgirl that needs tutoring? "Eight AM for the chat about Dash's Hollywood deal," he instructs. "I only have thirty minutes. I have an off-site meeting." With that, I am dismissed. "Go home."

Heat burns my cheeks, and I draw a calming breath that is barely calming at all. I decide right then that I could easily tuck my tail and run out of the door. I do the opposite. I march to his desk, stand in front of him and press my hands to the wooden surface. "I chose yes, not no. It was *a choice*. If I'd wanted to say no, you'd have stayed in your lane. There is a difference between A and B." I turn on my heel and march toward the door.

"Like there's a difference between being a bastard and acting like one?" he challenges.

I halt, fingers curling into my palm again. I spin around and face him. "Exactly. And for the record, you *are* a bastard, Tyler Hawk."

"Then we achieved something tonight. You finally understand me."

Indeed, I think, only even in this moment, as angry, hurt, and humiliated as I am, that thought feels flawed. For now, though, I open the door and exit to the hallway. But I do not go home. I will not run. I'm going back to the party just as soon as I make sure I'm not wearing my makeup on my forehead.

CHAPTER THIRTEEN

Bella

I enter the bathroom with my thoughts racing. He's a bastard, but Tyler's still my boss. I step in front of the mirror and take one look at my swollen lips and catch the edge of the counter. *Unless that changes tomorrow*, I think.

I shove aside that brutal thought with the same fierceness I all but begged Tyler not to walk away from me. Irritated at my line of thought, I shut down any negativity in my mind. I simply can't allow myself to go down the wrong rabbit hole, at least not when I'm here at the office. I know me, and if I do that, I will fall apart, even if only momentarily. With a need to be cool and composed, even if it's a façade of cool and composed, I quickly wipe away the lipstick on my chin, reapply a fresh pink shade, and fix the mess that is my finger fucked blonde hair. I try not to think how close I came to being wholly fucked by Tyler Hawk because I might as well have been. I had my leg on the man's shoulder and his mouth all over me. Okay, I'm going to freak myself out. It's time to leave.

I head for the door only to realize my nipple is not in my bra. Of course, it's not. I right the wrong, at least this one. There's no saving me from most of what I've allowed to happen, or as Tyler put it himself, the consequences, whatever they may be, of what I allowed to happen. Drawing a deep, calming breath, I pray Tyler is still in his office, and exit the bathroom. The coast appears clear, but I hurry to the elevator and punch the button over and over, glancing at the corporate office door several times as I do. As if either of those things will assure Tyler doesn't exit from the lobby before the elevator opens.

Finally, the car dings, the doors open, and I enter the elevator. I punch the rooftop button and hold my breath as I'm slowly sealed inside as if I'm in a horror movie and the monster might catch me. I'm fairly certain though I'm my own monster in this case because as Tyler said, I didn't say a proper no. I didn't say no at all. Once I'm secure and alone, I lean on the wall and let out a breath of relief, only to inhale the distinctly masculine scent of Tyler's cologne. He was just in the elevator, which means he either left the building or he's upstairs, where I'm headed. Lord, help me, but I'm not going to hide from this. I will see him again. I will face him again. I will hate him again. I will work with him again.

In the midst of this parade of sentences starting with "I will," Tyler's words play in my head. "*This is about control,*" he'd declared, and did so before I ended up mostly naked.

I'll analyze the real meaning of his claim to control later when I'm alone and can fully realize the tiny bubble of anger reforming inside me.

For now, there is another ding, and the doors to the elevator slide open. I straighten, exit, and leave behind the scent of Tyler, or so I think I do. Instead, the scent clings to me. It was never the elevator that smelled of Tyler. It was *me*. I quickly reach inside my purse, grab my perfume and douse myself with Chanel No. 5, hoping I don't choke anyone to death with the freshly sprayed perfume meant to hide the fact that I've had my boss all over me.

Having done all I can do to disconnect myself from Tyler, I hurry to the entrance of the rooftop entertainment area and pause a moment as I will my heart to calm. Only then do I rejoin the party. Once I'm in the midst of the festivities, as expected, there are still plenty of guests to be entertained and I had no business going home. I suppose Tyler simply believed I needed an escape, which he offered me in more than one way this night. My poor judgment actually earned me both an escape via an orgasm, and a prison in the aftermath I can never wash away, even when I no longer smell of the utterly sexy scent of Tyler Hawk. Nor do I think I will forget how good he was with his tongue.

Lord, help me, once again, with this line of thinking.

A waiter passes by, and I grab a glass of champagne and manage one sip when I end up chatting with the manager of a highly successful music producer. Patty is an attractive dirty blonde, in her mid-thirties, and quite likable. I have nothing to do professionally with Patty or her client, but we've chatted and enjoyed a few laughs together on occasion as we do now.

I've barely regained my composure after she's told me a story about a radio show she visited, and the DJ who pulled his pants down to show her his cock tattoo when I ask, "Was it at least an impressive tattoo?"

She snorts champagne. "No one but you would ask that. It was quite impressive, but he was married. I suggested he show it to his wife."

"Good decision," I conclude, when the sense of being watched has my gaze jerking right, only to find Dash and Allie watching me. My heart sinks. They were not supposed to be here tonight, and now I'm caged in more ways than one. I touch Patty's arm, instantly hyperaware of my touchy-feely self being a big fail with

Tyler. "My brother is here," I say. "I need to go talk Hollywood with him."

Patty's eyes go wide and whip around the room until they land on Dash. "Oh my God," she murmurs, refixing her attention on me. "I'm a huge fan. Can I meet him?"

Pride never fails me when people, especially famous people, react this way to Dash. "Of course," I assure her, motioning for her to follow me.

We head in that direction, and I'm actually fairly relieved with the potential distraction Patty offers from any conversation I might have with my brother. If I spend too much time with Dash, I'm going to blurt out details on the contractual dispute I'm having with the studio over his unsigned Hollywood contract. He will, in turn, react negatively and pull out of the whole deal and in Hollywood, that kind of action could end the project with everyone, even a project this magnificent. And that's not good for Dash. I don't care about me. I care about being his sister and failing him. Representing him has been a good and bad thing. I was able to hide his addiction to underground fighting and help aid his recovery, but I also feel tremendous pressure to never fail him.

I worry I'm about to do just that.

I worry he knows me well enough to read me like a room of his readers. I mean the entire reason my brother ended up famous was that he took real-life experiences at the FBI, hunting a known assassin, and turned them into fictional genius. He's smart and observant. He can read his sister. Patty and I join Dash and Allie, and I waste no time introducing them. It's not long until Patty is in full-on, drill-the-author-with-ten-thousand-questions mode.

Allie leaves Dash to his fangirl and creates a separate group with me. Allie is a brunette, beautiful, and similar in looks to the Allison who is now gone, killed by Tyler's father. She almost ended up another victim when her life mimicked Allison's to such an extent that she started looking for her. It sounds like a fictional storyline, but Dash's assassin keeps tabs on him, and that means his love life. The assassin who inspired his books saved Allie's life.

And killed Jack Hawk.

"You didn't come over for waffles this weekend," Allie points out. "I'm spoiled. I'm used to our weekend chats and the amazing waffles you make us."

It's a thing I started with Dash last year. I bought him a waffle maker and I show up every weekend to ensure it doesn't get dusty. It's been surprisingly fun to include Allie. She makes Dash happy. She makes him better. She gave him the strength to walk away from addiction and deal with his pain, which has a lot to do with loss and death on his side of the family.

Dash and I share a mother we lost five years ago, but not a father, sadly, because my father is amazing. His was not. He died recently. It was brutal for Dash. Again, there was Allie, lifting him up, holding him up, really.

"Tell me you missed me because you wanted to talk about your wedding. Tell me you set a date," I demand.

It's the wrong question to ask, and I find that out quickly when she says, "We want to have this Hollywood deal knocked out. We thought it was done months ago."

I recover quickly, focusing on Allie's job at Hawk Legal, the management of our annual charity benefit. "Speaking of Hollywood," I say, "I managed to get the studio to donate for this year's auction."

She perks up. "Really? Tell me all about it."

I detail the entire conversation with the studio head and all that was promised and she's beaming with excitement. "God, I love you, woman."

It's then that Patty walks away and Dash joins us, fixing me in a blue-eyed stare that says all without saying anything. He knows I'm avoiding him. "What's up, little sis?"

That's all he has to say. I'm ready to spill all when suddenly I'm saved, or not, depending on how you look at it.

Tyler joins what has come to be our little circle, standing between Dash and Allie and across from me. Now I have the two men I most want to avoid and yet can't seem to live without, up close and personal.

CHAPTER FOURTEEN

Bella

I meet Tyler's stare, not about to cower from my long-time boss, and one-time sexual exploit any more than I was willing to run when he told me to. "I thought you went home?" he challenges, right here in front of Dash and Allie. What the heck is he doing? Dash will lose his shit if he thinks there's something between me and Tyler.

"Why would she go home?" Dash asks. "What did I miss?"

I decide to walk into this as honestly as I can. "One of my clients hit on me. Tyler stepped in. It got ugly. He assumed I couldn't handle the situation, and things got heated."

Dash's brow lifts in surprise and he glances at Tyler. "I hope you kicked his ass."

"Right out of the door," Tyler assures him, "but as Bella stated so elegantly. It got ugly. I do believe she called me a bastard."

Allie catches my arm and gives me a disbelieving look. "He is a bastard," I state. "You know. I know it." I eye my brother. "You know it, too."

"Speaking of bastards," Tyler replies. "Jesse Bates is playing a show on Friday night. He's a dick but he's talented."

Allie lights up. "Oh my God. Yes, please." She eyes Dash. "You did this."

Dash wraps his arms around her. "Of course, I did it."

"Good thing the concert's Saturday," Tyler replies. "He wants me to play golf with him Saturday. I don't like the game. I don't like the man." He lifts his chin at Dash. "You want in?"

Dash laughs and downs the glass of whiskey in his hand. "I wouldn't miss that shit show for the world. When one of you kills the other, I have the plot for my next book."

I glance up to find Malcolm entering the room, looking big, broad, and country in jeans and boots, his dark hair slicked back and my eyes go wide. Considering Josh said Malcolm was out of town, my heart thunders in my chest and my eyes jerk to Tyler. He's talking to Dash, not even looking at me, and I whisper, "Tyler," with an insistent urgency.

His gaze jerks to mine and I say, "Malcolm just walked in and I beg you to please let me handle him. He's my client—"

"Who is supposedly out of town," he supplies. "At least that's what Josh told my secretary when he RSVP'd for the event."

"That's what he told me as well. Obviously, that was a lie. Please let me handle this."

He studies me a moment and then says, "Not this time, Bella." And then he backs out of the group and starts walking.

My fingers curl into my palms and I grumble frustrated words. I don't even look at Dash or Allie. I rotate out of the circle and catch up with Tyler right as he joins Malcolm, who is focused on me. "Josh told me what happened."

"Which was what?" Tyler demands.

"Tyler," I warn tightly.

Malcolm holds up a hand. "It's fine, Bella. He should be protective. Frankly, I respect the hell out of him for looking out for you." He gives Tyler a nod and refocuses on me. "Josh lost his brother a couple of months back. He's been acting a fool ever since, drinking way too much, and he's going into rehab. When he gets out, if you feel you can, he needs a second chance."

My heart twists with the idea of losing Dash and with the certainty that addiction can change who we are and how we act. I've seen it with Dash when he spirals, blames himself for too many things, and then hits the fight clubs. "The door is open," I say. "I'm sorry you had to come. He said you were traveling."

"I just got back from Paris, but my absence from the party was more like hiding in the studio trying to get out of a slump. I need to stay out of the public eye and just focus. All this Hollywood stuff seems to be in my head."

I know a few things about Malcolm. One being he likes fine whiskey. Another is that sometimes he needs to just come down a bit and talk through things. Maybe Tyler can be that for him. I know he's been there for Dash and known just the way—man to man—to snap him out of shit, and vice versa.

"You need to stop thinking so much," I say. "And I know just the way. You're a whiskey lover, right? Don't tell him I told you, but rumor is, Tyler stashes some pretty exclusive bottles in his safe."

Malcolm's lips curve and he glances at Tyler. "The word is out, man. What do you have?"

Tyler motions to the door and says, "Since the word is out, let's go take a look."

"That's what I'm talking about," Malcolm replies, his mood shifting, lighter now. He offers me his hand and when I accept, he catches my hand. "You, gorgeous lady, are always professional, sharp, and just killing it for my career. Thank you. And I'm deeply sorry."

"My pleasure. Now go relax and enjoy that whiskey. We'll talk next week about what's next for you." He kisses my hand, but there is nothing sexual about any of his affection. It's all country gentlemen, a language a girl in Nashville learns to understand.

Tyler motions to the door again, and Malcolm starts walking. Tyler lingers a second, his gaze warm on my face, when he says, "You owe me a bottle of whiskey when he gets a payday."

"No," I say. "You will owe me a commission."

He actually laughs and walks away, and those butterflies are back, where the bees should be. Because Tyler Hawk is a bastard. I'd best never forget that.

CHAPTER FIFTEEN

Bella

Thanks to Malcolm and Tyler, all Dash and Allie want to talk about is Josh and my honor. I swear Dash is so pleased with Tyler, I can't help but wonder what he'd think if he knew Tyler had been between my legs, but I don't go there. I won't go there. Ever. Again.

I think.

With the promise of pizza in their near future and an invite for me to join them, I send them on their way home. I swing by my office, grab my things, and meet Kelly, one of my fellow staffers, an attorney in the rights department, at the elevator. I'm thrilled to have the reinforcements in case Tyler shows up, and willingly hitch a ride downstairs with her. Kelly is new to her job and the firm, but a total sweetie with curly, red Nicole Kidman-esque locks. We chat about the party on the ride down.

Once we're in the garage, I hit the clicker on my shiny new blue Mercedes, bought compliments of my own hard work, not my father's bank account, or my inheritance, thank you very much. I'm proud of my father, but both he and my mother came from nothing. I wanted to prove I could do the same. I lived poor and fought hard to get to the secure place I am today, at only twenty-seven, three years before my goal of thirty.

Kelly groans as she approaches her car. "Nooooo! This cannot be happening."

I step left to see what is wrong and spy her flat tire. "If it's a run-flat tire you're all good, at least for the night."

"It's not. While those are ideal, no changing of the tire, it just becomes its own spare, my car is older and used. The tire is the old fashion in-the-trunk spare. I swear I bought a luxury model to impress, not be practical, which has proven to be a mistake that keeps on giving. It has one issue after another." She glanced at her watch. "It's late. Everyone will leave the party soon. Do you know how embarrassing it will be to change my tire, and have someone like Tyler Hawk show up and see me sprawled out on the ground?"

The elevator dings and I swear Kelly rotates, a mask of dread on her face as she waits on whoever is going to exit, the dread morphing to horror as Tyler appears. He spots us instantly and does that long-legged, arrogant, way-too-sexy walk that he walks.

He glances at me, a hint of something I can't read in his eyes before he surveys the tire. "You have a spare?" he asks her.

"Yes," she says. "I was about to put it on." She sets her things on the hood. "Just about to get to work."

"I'll change it," he says, indicating his briefcase. "Let me put this up." He extracts his keys from his pocket and clicks the locks on his silver Porsche, which is one of the expensive, elite ones, and my father would approve. He does approve. I'd snuck a picture and sent it to him once. Okay, more than one.

"I can do it," she says. "Thank you, though." She holds up her arms. "Girl power and all that stuff."

"My mother would disown me if I let you change your own tire," he assures her and he strides toward his car, leaving me a bit stunned by the comment about his mother. It hits me then, what has changed about Tyler, and my reaction to Tyler.

Since Dash crashed and burned not so long ago, Tyler has been around here or there, and I've seen a side to him that I didn't know existed. One that is human. One that wouldn't have done to me what he did tonight, and that little soft spot in my heart for him goes hard again.

Kelly turns to me. "I can't let him do this."

"You don't tell Tyler what to do or not do, believe me, I've tried. Take the help, but I should go so it won't seem like I'm watching him work."

Tyler is already headed this way, his jacket gone, his shirt stretched over a well-defined body, and approaching from behind Kelly. She is completely unaware of him as she grabs my arm and says, "Please don't leave me alone with him."

Tyler steps to our side and says, "Where are your keys?"

She looks like she might fight him but seems to think better. "I'll get them." She moves toward the car. Tyler steps closer to me. "Aside from keeping her from having a meltdown, it would be more appropriate if you stayed."

A million rebuttals rest on my tongue "It's too late for that" among others, but Kelly is back, holding up her keys. "Thank you so much for this."

Tyler eyes me, a question in his eyes that borders on a demand. "I'll be right here, making sure you do it right. You know my father taught me to change a tire when I was five."

Tyler's eyes light with amusement. "Feel free to backseat drive," he replies. "Just shout out what you want. I'll be down on my knees, doing the heavy lifting."

My cheeks heat and it's all I can do not to call him a bastard again, in front of Kelly. But I bite my tongue almost as hard as he did my lip earlier. I also decide that if he sticks his tongue in my mouth again, I'll bite his too. The problem is this man might just like it.

I fold my arms in front of me, and I eye Kelly. "Let's get us and him some coffee, shall we?"

"That's a great idea," she approves, clearly happy to place distance between us and him.

I walk closer to Tyler, who is indeed on his knees. "Bastard."

"I love it when you talk so dirty to me."

"We're going to get you and us coffee, mostly so I won't kill you and she won't melt down as you suggested."

"Good idea. It saves me your backseat driving too."

My hand balls in between us and he eyes it and me. "I can think of better ways to take your anger out on me than hitting me."

I ignore him and stand up, motioning to Kelly for us to head to the elevator. We take our time, chatting about Tyler, of course. "How do you get away with having such a debate with him?"

Debate?

I chuckle. "I make him money. Lots of it."

"Oh. Yes. That is a good plan. I clearly need to make him and me money."

After that she lets that topic sleep a good slumber. It's an explanation she can accept.

It's a half hour later when Tyler is still struggling with the tire. I kneel next to him and whisper a little trick my father taught me. He tries it and it works. "Good work, Ms. Bailey," he says softly, and I have no idea how my last name and the tire tip turned the air all crackling and heat filled, but I'm suffocating in this man.

I pop to my feet, and a few minutes later, Kelly is pulling away and I'm left standing there with Tyler. He turns to face me. "Malcolm and I talked for two hours, and I lined him up to be in the studio with Jesse Bates Saturday."

"What about golfing?"

"I managed to dodge that bullet. How did you know my whiskey collection would open him up and calm him down?"

"I never thought the whiskey would do the job. I thought you would. The way you did Dash."

"I pissed Dash off."

"When necessary. Not all the time."

He studies me for several beats, his eyes dark and unreadable. "Go home, Bella."

It rings like a warning, and I have a flash of that moment in his office when he dragged my skirt down and treated me like shit. That's all it takes. I rotate on my heels, and I don't stop until I'm inside my car and the engine is cranked.

I drive away and I know without looking he's standing there, watching me leave.

LISA RENEE JONES

CHAPTER SIXTEEN

Bella

Home is where the heart is usually refers to family, but my cute little two-story house in downtown Nashville is empty for me. Okay, it's not little. Just last year I bought a huge place, had it remodeled, and finally moved in six months ago. As if buying a huge home somehow validated my success and therefore created happiness. If it works for my father, it could work for me, had been my mentality, but as of late, I can see that he's alone too.

He loved my mother and not one of the women chasing him and his stardom has ever replaced her. What I missed in the big picture was how he lives for fast cars, fast women, and stays so busy he never feels the pain.

Only I didn't miss it at all. I copied his formula.

My job has controlled my life for years now, to the point that I now go to Dash's place for waffles to feel the bond of home and hearth. I feel alone when I enter my foyer, with no one to greet me, not even the pitter-patter of furry paws. I just worry that I travel too much and work long hours.

But I need my home to feel like home, and a furry child would help. Lord knows kids are not in my future any time soon. Dash was feeling the same things when he found Allie. My father does as well, even if he won't admit it. I wonder if Tyler does as well, which is sort of how I got into this mess. My choice to go to Tyler after his father died came from me watching Dash struggle with the loss of his estranged father. Family matters, and Dash, fortunately, had me and Allie to get him through that. Tyler is so like my father—shutting everyone out—that I thought he needed someone.

And maybe I was right, but I wasn't that person. He treated me like my father treats women, like a physical escape that allows him to hide from a more emotional connection. I am no one to him. I'm not sure why that bothers me. But it does. A little too much, which I tell myself is about me and whatever I'm feeling about life lately, not about him.

I need something to feel fulfilled.

Tyler Hawk is not that something. He is not my someone.

He's my boss. The end.

CHAPTER SEVENTEEN

Tyler

I can still taste her on my tongue.

Hot water runs over my body in the shower of my master bedroom, after rejecting a cold shower to combat my body's craving for Bella. A better option would have been to say screw the party going on above us and her brother in the building. I could have just bent her over my desk and fucked her right there in my office. No one would have known but us. Then I wouldn't be hard as a rock with my own cock in my hand.

I pump my cock with images of Bella in my mind. Those breasts. Her perfect, pink nipples. Her moans and sighs. The tight grip of her body around my fingers, all slick and hot for me. The shy way she refused to say what she wanted. The moment she finally said, "I want you to lick my pussy." She didn't say my name, though. I should have made her. God, to have her naked and on top of me.

My cellphone rings in the distance and I ignore it, pumping into my hand to an orchestra of Bella's moans and sighs until I jerk with the intensity of my release. When it's over, my damn phone is ringing again, and I curse, facing the wall and letting the water pelt me. Whoever it is can wait. My body calms, but I can't say I'm satisfied.

Fucking her would have been satisfaction.

How many times have I thought about fucking Bella? How many times did I remind myself she is forbidden? How many times did I walk away until I didn't? I curse and push off the wall, running my hand over my face. I don't have to ask why I didn't walk away from Bella tonight. I know. Nothing about what happened was about satisfaction.

Josh's hand on her body stirred an unfamiliar, uncomfortable anger in me. I've never been jealous in my life, but I was jealous tonight. I took her into my office knowing damn well what I was feeling, and the risk it represented. She is my employee. She is not for me, and I am not my father. I will not become my father.

I will not touch Bella again.

CHAPTER EIGHTEEN

Bella

I'm running late.

After Tyler told me not to be late, I seem to be trying to do just the opposite. I pull into the parking lot with ten minutes to spare, with no coffee down me. I cannot deal with Tyler Hawk this morning without any coffee. Thankfully, Hawk Legal has its own little restaurant and coffee shop I call our café. We even have our own app. I order coffee for me and Tyler as a peace offering I hope he doesn't end up wearing. It's doubtful, considering he controls my paycheck, but I'm human and fallible. As to how I know his drink, we've run into each other at Cupcakes and Books, a little bookstore down the road, that Dash favors for his little writing escape.

We both go there for Dash.

It's the place to corner him. And since he's always there on Thursday, it's probably where I'll be heading after this meeting with Tyler, to talk to him about this mess with Hollywood and his contract.

Setting aside that dreaded meeting, Tyler drinks a cinnamon mocha latte, just like me, which our café creates rather masterfully. Deliciously, too. We both have it recreated at Cupcakes and Books.

I kind of like the idea of this being his drink. It makes him a bit more human. And he is human, no matter how hard he tries to hide it. He's never watched a chick flick? I find that hard to believe. He just feels like he can't risk being human, as if being human is weak, but judging from how his father treated him, I know where that comes from. Jack Hawk taught his son to show no weakness.

And Tyler mastered the skill.

With two minutes to spare until my meeting with Tyler, I've unloaded my purse and briefcase in my office and make my way to the café. The cups are waiting on the counter, and I'm about ten seconds from securing them when I hear. "Bella."

At the sound of Josh's voice, my energy spikes, and I whirl around only to find him red-eyed and exhausted. He's been drinking. He must read my assumption on my face, because he says, "I haven't been drinking. Well, not this morning."

"How did you get back here?"

"The receptionist was trying to find you for me and sent me here to wait. I just came to apologize. I'm going into rehab, and yes, I know in showbiz rehab is everyone's way of sidestepping trouble, but that's not what is happening here. I just—" he scrubs his jaw. "I was an asshole, and my mother wouldn't be proud of me. I should have asked you to coffee because I *do* like you, Bella. I handled it all like shit." He throws his hand up to his sides. "I shouldn't have said that. I better leave." He turns to walk away.

He's nothing like the arrogant ass from last night this morning, and I can't say if that's an act or fear or real remorse. Nevertheless, I want to be a part of his solution, not his problem. That's who I am. That's why I like my job. I do well, but I do well because my clients do well.

I call after him. "I forgive you."

He turns and looks at me. "Yeah?"

"Yes. Be well, Josh. And when you are, we can make lots of magic together. *Work magic.*"

It's then, that I realize Tyler has entered the café and he's watching us, and I hate the way my pulse races and not with the idea of a potential confrontation but with his presence, with memories of his hands and mouth on my body. But truly I should be thinking about poor Josh, because Tyler is in his path to the door. I'd warn him but it's too late. Josh turns and takes several steps toward Tyler before he halts abruptly. I fret within myself, trying to decide if I should intervene, but Tyler talked with Malcolm last night about Josh. As long as Josh remains apologetic, he doesn't need me. If he doesn't remain apologetic, there is no saving him anyway.

Tyler closes the space between himself and the other man. Seconds tick into a minute at most, and then Josh is walking to the door. I have just a moment to drink Tyler in—tall, dark, and good-looking—so damn perfect in a fitted, pinstriped blue suit. He is all man, no question on that point, arrogance dripping from him. I melted for him, and how could I not?

There is not a single woman, and some married too, who wouldn't die to have that man between their legs.

I have a flashback to a morning at my father's place. I'd answered the door, and a pretty brunette had lost her shit and actually hit me. She'd been one of his many women. She'd hated me, the other woman. Of course, I wasn't the other woman at all, but my father had chuckled once he knew I was safe and well, and said, "I don't even know her name."

Suddenly I feel dirty.

Tyler's gaze locks with mine, his awareness of my inspection evident in his stare, heat in the depth of his gaze...too much heat. Anyone watching has to notice. I whirl around, grab the coffees, and by the time I'm facing forward, he's towering over me again. "You're late," he says.

"Yes, but—"

"Yes," he insists, in typical, intolerant Tyler mode.

It's this attitude that pushes people away and I'm fine with being back in that little box again.

"*Yes*," I concur, "I am late, but I also got you coffee." I offer him one of the two cups.

He reaches for it, our hands brushing in the process, and I feel that touch in that spot between my legs where he's licked me. It's insane and unnerving. I don't like it. I'm that girl, that nameless girl, and it still feels just as dirty as before this touch.

Tyler's eyes narrow on me, his mouth curving in this ridiculously satisfied way, as if he knows I reacted to his touch. For a moment, I think he thinks I'm ready to lift my leg again, until he adds, "Just couldn't stomach me without caffeine now, could you?"

"That's actually the exact thought I had this morning," I confess, relieved that he's read me accurately.

His lips curve as if I've amused him but he's already past the moment.

He glances at his watch, a ridiculously expensive Breitling, with a black band, rose gold, and a touch of green on the otherwise black face. I know the watch because my father has a thing for watches and owns several Breitlings. I also know Jack Hawk wore a Rolex. I wonder if that is why Tyler does not. "I have to go. We'll talk when I get back." And he literally turns around and walks toward the door. This is not what I need from Tyler right now. In fact, all I've gotten from Tyler is a fight and an orgasm. That's not enough. I rush after him.

CHAPTER NINETEEN

Tyler

I've just stepped onto the elevator when Bella appears in the entryway using her slight frame to block the door's progress as it attempts to shut, the pale blue dress she's wearing hugging her curves.

"Oh, thank God," she gushes. "I gambled you'd come straight here and won. I really have to talk to you. I'll ride down with you." She joins me inside the car, and she turns her attention to the keyboard, punching the already lit lobby button, a sure sign she is as nervous as I am agitated with the both of us right now. I swear to God, she tests my vow not to touch her again just by existing.

The doors close and at this point, we're sealed inside the car, just the two of us, and between that dress on her banging body and the scent of her perfume, my cock is at attention. That part of my body would like very much to fuck her against the elevator wall or anywhere else, for that matter, but that's not going to happen, not with Bella. Because my fantasies about Bella are not fantasies at all when they lead to a place where she is broken, even if she leaves me bloody in the process. Which may well be her true intent now. "Say your piece, Bella."

She glances over at me. "I'll wait until we're out of the car. I'm paranoid about cameras."

In other words, this urgent matter remains about Dash, not last night. As for the cameras, she's not paranoid. We represent some of the biggest talents in the world, including her brother. The floors tick by and she fidgets with her perfectly manicured hands twisting in front of her, a nervous habit that isn't a habit at all. Bella doesn't fidget. Except now. With me. The elevator is quick about its job and the doors open at lobby level.

I hold the door and motion Bella forward. She steps outside into the lobby and rotates to wait on me. When I exit and keep walking toward the elevator leading to the garage, she quickly falls in step with me. "There's a new studio head with a reputation for killing big projects before they hit the red carpet."

Fuck, I think, but what I say is, "How new?"

"Three weeks."

We pause at the elevator bank, and I punch the garage-level button. "And I'm just now hearing this?"

"Week one seemed as balmy as a beach day. Week two turned to winter. Week three, which is now, is going straight to hell."

The elevator doors open. I motion her forward and step inside, biting back a few rather critical questions with those cameras still at the core of my silence. Instead, I punch the proper button, and Bella joins me. She glances over at me and solemnly says, "It's bad, Tyler."

Probably not a bad as she thinks, I remind myself. This deal is personal for her because of Dash, and an overreaction to a negative turn in negotiations is natural. That type of connection to a deal this big hypes every potential problem to new levels, which I know well because I worked for my father most of my adult life. And my father made sure the board felt as if I worked all for them, and just them. It was brutal but it did shape me into the man I am today. And that man knows how to run this operation.

The elevator dings again and the minute the doors open, Bella hurries out and into the garage. turning to wait on me again. The minute I join her she says, "He's stripping the contract. Dash lost his role as a scriptwriter and no longer has casting approval."

"Tell them that's unacceptable."

"This is me, Tyler. Do you really think I didn't push back? This guy is not moving. And I could get one of these things past Dash, but not both. I haven't told him any of this is going on. I know him. He'll pull out, and I've heard stories of this studio head. He goes after those who wrong him, and everything that doesn't go his way has a wrong attached."

"The studio isn't going to be stupid enough to lose Dash."

"This is Hollywood, not Nashville. These people walk away from massive money all the time."

"What about the second studio that was bidding on the deal? Can you go back to them and leverage two studios against each other?"

"I made the foolish mistake of telling one of the studio execs how much Dash hates the other studio, as in everything about them. They didn't sit right with him creatively." I hold up a hand. "In my defense, I thought the deal was done. I now know it's never done until it's playing on screens." She waves me onward. "Now tell me how stupid I am because I know. Believe me, I know."

It wasn't smart, but Bella is anything but stupid. "How close to falling apart?"

"Seconds. And I'm scared, Tyler. I can't screw this up for Dash. Or you. All things aside, this company has been good to me. You trusted me with very little experience and here I am, proving that as a risk."

She's scared. Those words have never come out of Bella's mouth, at least not to me. And I know why. It's about family, something she values, and I generally tolerate. I get along with my mother, but she lives in her own world, not one that is shared with anyone else, including me. She's still in Europe and her portion of the will has been read, while mine has waited months to finally be revealed this morning. I don't even know when the fuck my mother is coming back to the States, or if she's coming back at all.

"I can't fail, Dash," Bella says, dragging me back to the moment.

"You're letting emotion and fear win, which is not like you. Step off the ledge, Bella, unless you intend to jump into the shark-infested waters and get eaten alive."

"I have no strategy at this point, no angle to work."

"Objectively, do you feel your personal involvement has impacted the deal negatively?" I ask, forcing her to see what I already know. She's the best thing Dash has on his side.

"I've analyzed myself over and over," she replies, "and I don't think I'd do anything differently with another client. I feel like my connection to Dash has pros and cons. The pros...I know Dash. I know what he will say yes or no to. I influence him and calm him. The con is that I don't want this to fall apart, and they know it."

"No agent wants this kind of deal to fall apart." I glance at my watch and I'm already late for this reading. "I have to go. Text me the studio head's name. Let me call in a few favors and get the inside scoop on him."

"I think I need a second hand in this, a good cop, bad cop kind of situation. And you do the bad cop so well." Her cheeks flush and I know why.

We both clearly remember the whole "*Am I bad?*" thing from last night. The fact that the memory only makes me want to show her how bad I really am by lifting her skirt and licking her all over again is not working toward the whole never touching her again vow.

"I need to go. I'll come find you this afternoon when I get back to the office." I start to turn, and Bella catches my arm. My gaze lands searchingly on her face and she jerks her hand back.

"I'm sorry. I told you the touching thing is a thing for me."

"Just never with me."

"Because the desk is always between us," she says, her voice soft, free of confrontation, but there is a vulnerability to her in that moment that reminds me she is human, sweet, and caring. Things I can never be. I will hurt her if either of us gives me the chance.

"I'm just being me," she says, "and—"

"Then go with that, Bella. Be you and you will win, which means Dash will win." I turn away from her and start walking before I'm the one who touches her this time. Because I have more than a little to communicate with Bella, all of it naked.

LISA RENEE JONES

CHAPTER TWENTY

Tyler

The offices of Jones, Jackson, and Withers are only a mile from Hawk Legal.

By the time I'm pulling into the parking garage of the building, I have a text message from Bella waiting on me. *Michael Sumner is the new CEO,* her message reads. *And thank you again, Tyler.*

It's an impersonal message but everything with Bella feels personal these days, including Michael Sumner threatening Dash's deal. Ironically, and outside the taboo employee situation, Dash is a friend who has known me at my worst. He'd never want me with Bella and most likely we'd come to blows. Because he'd never think me good enough for her and he wouldn't be wrong.

I forward the new studio head's name to Dierk Jordan, who is my fix-it guy. Dierk is ex-special ops, turned CIA. He retired when something he calls "dirty" pushed him too far. It must have been really fucking dirty, because Dierk likes his work dirty. He does what no one else can do. Just for good measure, I also send the name to Reid Archer, my CFO at Hawk Legal, and a former classmate at Yale. We lost touch for seven years and one day, I walked into a meeting with a financial firm, and he was there. It was clear his knowledge of most things reached beyond our years.

One piece of advice my father gave me rings true: surround yourself with people who know more than you, and you'll create a winning team. You'll also eventually know what they know, if you make the effort to ensure you learn from them.

Reid is one of those people, and I credit myself for bringing him on board at Hawk Legal. In his area of expertise, he knows more than me. When I learn what he knows, he tops his experience off with more experience and more knowledge. And he's proven to me time and time again that he'll use that knowledge to my benefit. I take good care of Reid. He takes good care of me. And I trust Reid when I trust only a few people.

A few minutes later, I'm sitting in a private office lined with books, expensive paintings, and enough new-smelling leather to suffocate me and everyone else who visits. If I'm going to get drunk on a smell, I'd rather it be Bella's sweet, floral scent, no matter how damn hard it gets me. Not the preferences of my father's attorney sitting across me, studying documents he should be explaining to me.

Withers is an older man, with thick gray hair and ten years on my father, though he's still fit and able-bodied despite the cast that speaks to his recent skiing accident. He is, or was, my father's Reid. My father trusted him. I'm not sure that plays out well in my favor, but then nothing in the will my father wrote can be changed at this point. It is what it is. The words are written in stone unless I go to court and unwrite it, and that's a tough, public battle. Exactly why I pray my father did right by me in death when he never did right by me in life.

With a tap-tap of the upright folder on the table, Withers clears his throat and fixes his stare on me. His eyes are thick with what I can only call dread. I am not going to like what he has to say, nevertheless, I have to hear it.

"Just get to it," I urge.

"I know this process has been uniquely structured, but I do want to assure you your father had a logical purpose for the delay."

A muscle in my jaw tics at the ridiculous statement. Logic was never the motivation my father used when punishing me, which was a daily ordeal. "And that would be what?"

"He wanted you to have time to emotionally cope with his death before you took on the challenges he's made to your role as his successor."

Of course, my father couldn't give two fucks about my emotional recovery or anything resembling my well-being. "Elaborate," I order softly. "And do so quickly."

He slides a piece of paper in front of me. "Your mother split the cash in the bank with you for the sum of five hundred million each. I'll need you to fill out a wire transfer form." He slides the paperwork in front of me.

I fill out the form. The money isn't unexpected, though I have my own. I've invested well. I've prepared to be cut out of the family fortune. I complete the document and hand it back to the other man and do so with no sense of relief. There is a heaviness in the air, a seemingly illogical expectation I read in Withers that a man that just inherited five hundred million dollars is about to be an unhappy one.

He studies the document I've handed him and then glances at me. "The wire will go out today. This sum of money will take some time."

"I understand. Move on."

"Yes. Moving on. Your mother is out at Hawk Legal, which she agreed to in advance. You're the sole inheritor of your father's stock and therefore the controlling financial partner, with a few conditions.

These conditions must be met within fourteen months of his death. He felt you needed a full year after the reading of the will to enact his demands."

Demands. The word says it all.

This is going to be another mind fuck by my father. I know this all too well without one extra detail, but I still provide the expected response. "What conditions?"

"It's spelled out in the documents in the folder. Let me leave you to look it over and digest the details. After which, I'll return and make myself available to answer questions." He stands up, exits the room, and shuts the door. It's fairly obvious he didn't want to take the brunt of my reaction. He wants me to cool down before he deals with my "questions."

My cellphone rings and I snake it from my pocket to find Dierk's number on caller ID. I answer the call because what's in the folder can't be changed. The outcome of Dash's Hollywood deal still has hope. "What do you have for me?" I ask.

"That new CEO has a reputation for killing deals. What existed before he takes over never survives. If you don't want his deal to die, leverage him, or take it elsewhere."

"Leverage him with what?"

"There's a cloak-and-dagger situation related to why he left his last studio. I'm digging. What I do know is that there was one exception to his kill program for existing projects. He hates to lose a bid and he held onto one script to keep it from going to another studio."

"Did he make the project?"

"Yes. It was *Starlight.*"

One of last year's biggest films. "At least he knows how to go big. Get me that cloak and dagger data."

"More soon," he says, and he disconnects.

I return my attention to the folder and like all bad things, I don't wait and see. I rip the Band-Aid off. I open the folder and stare at the envelope sitting on top of a document, that reads "Tyler" in my father's print.

Tyler–

Here is how this plays out.

You inherit my stock and become controlling partner, but there's a catch. If you do not meet the guidelines of my will, the stock will revert evenly to all partners, excluding you. To secure your stock, and solidify it as yours and yours alone, you must marry within a year of this letter. On the eve of your wedding, my legal team will officially transfer your inheritance in full.

Additionally, you must put on a show and carry on an extended engagement in the public eye. At least six months to look respectable. You better make it look good, boy. My logic is sound. At this point, Hawk Legal needs stability and a family man as a leader. It will not survive my departure without a moral leader, which I have not been. No need for details. You know enough. You'll discover the rest. Make this work. Or don't. I'm dead. You are the one who has to live with my consequences now, not me. I told you to marry long ago, to establish a certain reputation, and you ignored me. Now you will not.

Goodbye, Tyler.

Oh, one more thing…

If you fail, you get one million, not five hundred million. The rest goes to a charity of your choice, but of course, without any connection to you at all.

LISA RENEE JONES

CHAPTER TWENTY-ONE

Tyler

I'm reeling with my father's words.

I grab the form I'd filled out where it still rests on the table. Withers has not filled in the transfer amount.

The door opens and I pop to my feet, expecting Withers, but instead, it's his secretary, Tabitha, a middle-aged brunette with a no-nonsense attitude. "Mr. Withers had an emergency and he realized he forgot to give you a document. He believes it's quite important." She hands it to me and hurries away. In a blink, the door is shut again.

I open the document and curse. Inside, I find the detailed account of a case I was dragged into years ago as co-council to my father. He broke laws to protect a client and cover up crimes. I was told they would kill us if we crossed them. My father also assured me that if I opened my mouth, I'd be disinherited. Now, it's come back to haunt me. There is a sticky note—a damn sticky note—attached to the documents, with another note written in my father's script. *"Son, don't be stupid. The minute you take my will to court, this goes public. I don't give two bleeps what it does to Hawk Legal. I'm dead."*

And I'm buried, I think.

He was ruthless.

He's ensured I have two options.

I either marry or walk away from my birthright.

My cellphone rings again and I glance at the caller ID. It's Bella. I answer the line. "Yes, Bella?"

"The studio head wants to see me tomorrow afternoon. I hate to put you in this position, but I think I need my bad cop along for the ride."

Bella wants me to travel to LA with her, which in my present state of mind is not a safe proposition for her but right now, I don't give two shits. "I'll pick you up at your place at three. We'll fly out tonight."

"Okay," she says. "I, uh—Tyler, we—"

"Have business to attend, Bella. I'll pick you up at five." I disconnect and sit there a moment, processing what just happened. And I think of Bella. I think about Bella way too much for the good of either of us. I glance down at the folder and open it again, giving the document another read-through and finding no escape clause. "That bastard," I bite out, accepting the inevitable,

I dial the third person in my armory of trusted allies, Gavin McCloud, my attorney. "I need a contract drawn up."

CHAPTER TWENTY-TWO

Bella

The minute I hang up with Tyler, I shut my door, lean against the hard surface for stability, and draw in a deep, calming breath that doesn't calm me at all. The problem is that my door reminds me of *his* door, and the naughty things he did to me against it. This trip, which, no doubt amounts to me and him together in an intimate setting at least a few times, is dangerous. Tyler knows this, too. I know he knows. Neither of us believes what happened between us was right, which I'm sure is why he so harshly dismissed me.

At least he waited until, after my orgasm, I think a bit bitterly, considering how horribly he treated me. It wasn't necessary. But setting aside my personal feelings that have no more room in this situation than did our behavior, I focus on the reason for this trip. Obviously, Tyler found out something about the new studio head or he wouldn't believe this trip a necessary evil. He must have found out something about the new studio head. At this point, I have to assume that Dash's deal is really in danger. And I can't in good faith hide these negotiations from my brother. I love him too much to end up shocking him with a crisis.

Decision made, I push off the door and straighten with determination. He'll be at the coffee shop. It's time to talk to him and confess my worries.

I load up my briefcase, grab my coat and purse, and head for the door. Once I'm in the Hawk Legal lobby and headed toward the elevator, Morgan, the new receptionist, a pretty twentysomething blonde, calls out to me, "Bella!"

Halting, I backstep with the realization I haven't even told the team I'm leaving and won't be back for a few days. I rotate and close the space between me and Morgan, already anticipating what might come next. "Please tell me I don't have a problem to solve."

"Oh, no. Nothing is wrong. I just wanted to apologize for letting Josh back in the cafe today. I had no idea he was a problem."

It's then that I realize I didn't even ask Tyler what happened between the two men. Not that I think Tyler really gave me the chance, but he also didn't confront me about Josh showing up to speak to me either. I make a mental note to ask Tyler exactly what was said between him and Josh, because I don't seem to be fully abreast of the situation.

For now, I focus on Morgan. "He's not a problem. He's simply working through a few things, and he came to apologize for allowing that to overflow into his work. Also, I'm heading to LA for a few days. I'm leaving this afternoon, so please take messages and forward them to me. I will still be working for my clients when I'm gone."

"Of course," she agrees. "Please let me know if I can do anything to help. Honestly, I'd love to be considered for the assistant position I saw posted, working for you directly."

I'd almost forgotten that I've graduated to a place in the firm where I've been allotted my own assistant but have had little time to interview. This is because I need an assistant. Oh, the irony. But perhaps Morgan is making this simple for me. The reception spot is often the place where we try people out and promote them and so far, Morgan has been excellent. "Let's chat when I get back," I suggest.

"That would be great. Let me know if I can play that role while you are gone. Anything you need, I'm here." She hands me a piece of paper. "My phone number."

"Text it to me. I'm too scattered right now. I will 100% lose it."

"You bet," she says. "And I'm an excellent organizer. You will never lose anything with me on your side."

"I love it. Talk soon. I need to go now, though."

"Good luck in LA."

"I might need it. Thank you."

I walk away from her, thinking about how far I've come at Hawk Legal, and how far I could fall if I end up in bed with Tyler. Not that I think he intends any such thing, not after the horrible way our encounter ended, but the weird sexual chemistry between us was not gone this morning. I don't want any of this to get out and affect the perception of my abilities. The whole office would think I slept my way to the top, and for who? A man who will never want more than sex. And I do. I'm at that point in my life where I think I'm done with random, useless relationships that really amount to flings.

It's time to get back to work and back to business in all ways, especially with my boss.

But I'm really not as angry with him now as I was last night. The truth is, he's vulnerable after his father's death, and in ways, he'd never admit or probably even see in himself. He doesn't really want or need sex. He needs a friend, but he's afraid of the connection. Sex is just the way he hides from anything real. I need to show him I'm safe. He can trust me without any reason to find a way to divide us.

He doesn't have to fuck me until I hate him and walk away.

Friends don't walk away from each other.

They stand by you.

CHAPTER TWENTY-THREE

Bella

The bells chime as I open the door to Cupcakes and Books. By the time I walk into the cozy, deliciously scented bakery side of the establishment, I'm no longer fretting over my conversation with Dash. Truly, I think I've worked myself up into this frenzy out of fear of letting him down when that is unnecessary. I won't let him down. I will always lift him up in any way possible and he knows this. Just as I know he will always do the same for me.

My gaze immediately seeks out Dash, and as expected, I find him well settled in at his favorite corner table, busy at work, his attention focused on his computer screen. Adrianna, one of the store owners—a tall, gorgeous, woman who is probably in her late forties, but I swear she looks thirty-five—waves to me from behind the counter. "Your normal?" she queries.

My normal is a quiche, followed by a cinnamon mocha latte in a mug, and a strawberry cupcake. The mugs really give this place a cozy touch. "Yes, please!" I call out, offering her a friendly smile. I like her. I like her husband, Jackson, too, wherever he is right now. This place is one of those places that makes you feel like you're home and every holiday baking season, makes you wish for the next. Truly, the tasty-themed creations found inside these walls never fail to please.

I head toward my brother's table, but I'm intercepted. A woman with bouncy red curls is fawning all over him, and he seems to be signing a book for her.

My brother is both good-looking and talented. Women love him and I don't know how Allie takes the attention he receives, but maybe she just knows he loves her. I certainly do. He was a loner until he met her, so like my father, you'd have thought they were of the same blood. But I've said the same of Tyler, so I suppose it's just a single-guy thing.

I halt and stall my approach, allowing Dash's fan a bit of time with him until she reluctantly backs away from his table. Dash's eyes land on me and he smiles, and it's a smile that proves how different he is since Allie came into his life. I didn't see the hollowness of his smiles in the past. But now I do. Now, I see that this smile reaches his eyes and lights his face. I truly believe his happiness with Allie is part of the reason I'm feeling alone. I haven't lost Dash. But I haven't fully found myself, either.

I claim the seat across from him and he shuts his computer and sets it on the chair to his right. "What's up, little sis?"

"You tell me," I urge. "How's the new book coming?"

"It's actually flowing. Life feels calmer. It's working for me."

"Since Allie came along," I assume.

"Yes," he agrees. "Since Allie came along, but enough about me. There's been too much of that lately."

He's not talking about his career. He's talking about his fighting, and the battle we all fought to end that part of his life.

"The event seemed like it went well last night," he observes.

"It did. People seem happy to have Tyler running the show."

"If Jack treated staff and clients anywhere near as badly as he did Tyler, I'm not surprised. Any idea how Tyler is doing?"

"He's Tyler. No one has any idea how he's doing, which probably means he's suffering. He needs you. You're the only one he seems to talk to."

"Not any time as of late. I've tried."

"Try harder, Dash. Maybe just show up at his place?"

"That's really not a bad idea. I'd say I'd grab an expensive bottle of whiskey and take it over there to share with him, but he drinks too damn much."

It's not the first time Dash has made that reference and there was a whiskey glass on the table when I visited Tyler, but the idea of him spinning out of control with that type of addiction doesn't sit right. "He never had a glass in his hand at the party last night. It seems like if he had an addiction, he would have. And do control freaks become addicts?"

"You're talking to me, Bella. Yes, we do, and when we fall, we fall hard."

Adrianna sets my plate in front of me and a diet drink as well, because she knows me. The diet first. The coffee next. We chat with her for a moment before it's just me and Dash again. "Back to Tyler," Dash says. "Maybe I'll go by his place this weekend."

"He's out of town this weekend, Dash." I slide my plate aside. "I need to talk to you."

He narrows his eyes on me. "Why so serious?"

"There's a new studio head. He's trying to make changes to your contract you won't like. I'm pushing back and he's not budging."

"I see," he says. "Go on."

"I think the deal could fall apart. We need to go back to the competing studio and really consider them as a viable option. This will create a fresh bidding war between studios A and B, A being your preferred studio. But you have to be willing to move studios if we play that card."

"You know how I feel about the studio head at B."

"He rubbed you wrong. I get that. And when this was an apples-to-apples thing, that was a fine way to pick your studio. If what you want is spelled out in a contract, then you're protected. And you never have to deal with A or B. I will. I just need you to say yes to how I want to approach this. We need to protect your future and when things go south in Hollywood they sometimes, more times than they should, die. Even projects as big as yours. Please open your mind."

He studies me a long moment, and then says, "You're really worried this is going to fall apart." It's not a question. He's reading me a like a book.

"Enough that I'm going to LA this afternoon. Hollywood can offer you a changing opportunity, Dash. If this opportunity falls apart, I want you to know that I fought for you like I'm fighting for my own life and yours."

"I know you will, Bella. And if falls apart, it falls apart. Do I need to go with you?"

"No. I think it's better if they feel you're removed and unemotional about any of this. Tyler's going with me."

"Tyler," he says flatly, "is going with you. As in, just the two of you?"

"Yes," I confirm, and I just ignore the accusation of his statement and move on as if it didn't just pop me right in the jaw. "I had an idea that we'd play a good cop, bad cop strategy with the studios. I asked for his help. He's skilled and his experience—"

"I'm sold on you two as a team, but that's not the point, now, is it?"

"What is the point, Dash?"

"Allie said she sensed something between you last night. And you have been fretful over him. You went to his place a couple times to check on him?"

"Just once," I say, though he's right. I dropped by two other times, and he wasn't home. Seems I was determined to wade into shark-infested waters, just as Tyler referenced.

I'm determined to get eaten alive.

LISA RENEE JONES

CHAPTER TWENTY-FOUR

Bella

I'm lost in my own self-reflection and persecution when Dash snaps me back to the present. "And?" he challenges. "What happened when you went to Tyler's apartment, Bella?"

"I forced him to eat ice cream and he forced me to leave afterward."

He laughs. "You forced *Tyler Hawk* to eat *ice cream?*"

"Oh, come on. Everyone loves ice cream. It was nothing and nothing happened."

"What about what Allie sensed?"

"He's been weird with me since I took him that damn ice cream. He doesn't seem to know how to be friends with a woman. I think it scares him, but you know it's for the best. He's my boss, not my friend. I should never have forgotten that."

"Why did you?"

"That's easy to answer. When you lost your dad, Dash, you struggled but even so, you had me and Allie. He has no one. It's that bleeding heart of mine. I think I felt like he was my friend because he's your friend."

He just stares at me a moment, as if he reads more into the answer than I thought was there. Finally, he asks, "Why didn't you come have waffles this past weekend?"

"It wasn't about Tyler, that's for sure. I didn't want to tell you the contract was falling apart, Dash. I didn't want to let you down."

"Are you serious? You stayed away because of *that*?"

"Yes. I just wanted to pull it all together and tell you everything was great."

"Good, bad, and ugly, Bella. That's you and me forever. Don't hide things from me. I did from you, and look where I ended up. In underground fight clubs."

"And maybe Tyler ends up drowning in a bottle, Dash. If you're right and he has a problem, we have to help him."

"What happened to my boss, not my friend?"

My lips purse. "Okay, *you* have to help him. I have to step back from it."

"You're right. You do. Because I do not want you ending up in bed with Tyler Hawk, because as you said, your bleeding heart got involved, and thought that's what he needed at the time. He has a 'fuck me tonight' address book ten miles long."

"I don't need this particular lecture. You know that, right?"

"I think you do. I sense it, Bella, and so did Allie. Be careful with Tyler." He slides my plate in front of me. "And eat your lunch. You need the energy to negotiate my contact."

My phone buzzes with a text and I snake it from my purse to find Tyler, of all people, on my ID. I click the message and read: *I'll text you when I'm ten minutes from your place. I need your address.*

I sent him the information and the exchange ends there. I set my phone down on the table and Dash arches a brow. I pick up my fork. "Tell me about the book you're writing."

"There's no story to tell right now. It's too soon."

A little like me and Tyler, I think. We are nothing more than a few lines on the page, or perhaps one paragraph.

Hardly worthy of Dash's warning of *"Be careful with Tyler."*

Yet hours later, those words ring in my head as I finish packing and wait on Tyler to pick me up. I clearly lied to Dash when I told him I didn't need his lecture. We both knew better. In fact, I've been thinking about Dash's warning and my actions with Tyler for hours.

I am not going to sleep with Tyler Hawk.

The idea that he has an address book ten miles long actually sickens me a bit. I can't help but wonder how many women he's shoved against a door. Maybe he can promise a grand orgasm because he has lots of experience. He's a manwhore. He likes it that way. Let him keep on living his own way. On his own. Alone.

The doorbell rings, and my brows furrow. I'm not expecting a delivery, and according to a text message from Tyler about two hours ago, he'll text me when he's outside waiting on me. Maybe I do have a delivery I forgot. I hurry toward the door and when I fling it open, I suck in a breath. Tyler is standing there, right in front of me, in jeans and a snug, long-sleeved sweater that hugs his muscular torso. Our eyes collide and just that easily, I'm tingling with awareness. Dash's lecture will not save me. There's no escaping Tyler Hawk. Not anymore. Something has changed between us, really it had changed long before the office door incident, and there is no turning back.

LISA RENEE JONES

CHAPTER TWENTY-FIVE

Bella

I quell my nervous energy and force myself to face this moment as if it were any other, not one where my boss who has been between my legs is at my front door. "What are you doing here, Tyler?"

"I thought you might need help with your luggage."

"I'm not even done packing. You were supposed to text me ten minutes before you got here and you're twenty minutes early."

"Invite me in and I'll wait."

My brows dip. "Is this payback for me showing up at your door unannounced?"

"I'm not unannounced. You knew I was coming. Invite me in, Bella." His voice is a low command with a raspy, almost intimate quality.

I hesitate and then ease back onto the foyer, folding my arms in front of me, as if that will stop my breasts from aching simply because he's in my presence.

"There's Diet Coke and baked Cheetos in the kitchen, but not much," I say flippantly, as if he would eat a baked Cheeto, or at least admit to it. "Make yourself at home. Not really. Just sit somewhere. I have to finish getting ready." But I don't immediately step away. I'm suddenly wondering what he sees when he sees my home. Beyond this room, my living area has vaulted ceilings with wooden beams and a stunning chandelier I still love since I had it installed two years ago. My furniture is a mix of brown and white linens, while my fireboard is this magical, dark wooden masterpiece. The kitchen, which overlooks the living area, is a mix of wood and white marble. It's a beautiful place, of that I know, but what does it *say* about me?

Alone with nothing to do but decorate, I think.

"Bella?" Tyler questions.

"Yes?" I mentally shake myself and motion behind me, telling him where to go wait, as I've instructed. "I'm going upstairs. You stay here."

His eyes light with what appears to be amusement. My discomfort amuses him. This doesn't surprise me one little bit. "You should hurry," he encourages. "We're flying commercial. I thought you'd be more comfortable that way."

"I'm not sure what that means," I say flatly.

"That way you don't have to be alone with me," he replies.

"Like I am now?" I challenge, somehow offended by the idea that he chose to place a barrier between us. I've known the man for years. We have been alone many times without any hands on each other. We probably aren't even sitting together. Maybe he's in first and I'm in coach. That will teach me to bring him ice cream.

"We have a flight to catch." He glances at his watch and then at me. "You have ten minutes to get ready or we might be flying private anyway."

Whatever, I think. He's really a bastard, and I don't analyze why that's the thought I have right now. It just is. All the analyzing of myself objectively is out the door when he's inside my house. I cut my gaze and hurry up the stairs, which wind left and then right before I'm on the top level. My room is to the right. Once I'm inside the solitude of my private space, I cross to the bed where my suitcase lies open and grab one of the large posts framing my mattress just trying to catch my breath. My heart is thundering against my breastbone and my stomach is back to the whole somersault routine. I also swear I smell like Tyler all over again, and that's impossible. This time, he hasn't touched me to leave a lingering impact. *But I want him, too*, I think. God, I want him too, and I am in so much trouble right now. Why I would pick my boss to get this worked up over, I don't know. And after all these years working with him, why now?

God.

Tyler is here, in my home. I never thought I'd see that day, but maybe he felt the same about me in his. Maybe I deserve to be rattled like this. *Shake it off, Bella*, I command myself. Shake it off. He's waiting on me. A plane is waiting on us. Hollywood needs a big kick in the pants by both of us. I got this. I have control. Of course, I do. I have managed famous actors and singers and waded through treacherous waters working with many an arrogant executive. Those suits are the worst. They have the real power. If I handled them, which I did, I can handle one equally arrogant man I've known my entire career at Hawk Legal.

I'm about to seal up my bag when I realize that I'm presently in my work clothes and Tyler is not. I need to know how to dress and what to expect when we get to LA. How have I asked nothing about what is on the agenda? *Because you're too busy lusting after his body*, I chide myself. I'm being silly and inappropriate when I should be professional.

I rotate to hunt Tyler down, only to gasp as I find him leaning one big shoulder on the inside of my doorframe. I don't smell like Tyler. He's here, smelling up my room with bad intent, and hot man.

"What are you doing in my room?" I demand.

"Seems you now understand how I felt when I found you in mine." It's not a question.

"I was in your bathroom."

"Attached to my bedroom you had to pass through."

"I had to pee," I argue, "and that bathroom by the door you mentioned was not easy to see. I never saw it."

"You didn't look very hard."

"*I had to pee,*" I repeat. "When a girl has to pee, she has to pee. I had a reason for entering your room. What is yours visiting mine?"

"I could tell you I just wanted to ensure you packed for a long stay, but I'm not one to play games, Bella. The truth is you saw my room. I wanted to see yours."

I open my mouth to say, "you saw a whole lot more of me than I did you," but quickly press my lips together before I regret where I take this. As for my room, it's my space, my private sanctuary with a massive four-poster bed, a cozy chair, a bench, and lots of creams and blues. It's for me, not for him, but he's not going to leave because I insist that he leaves, so I don't bother to push. "What did you mean pack for an extended stay? Do we have meetings set-up?"

"I set an appointment with the new studio head for tomorrow at three. From what my insider tells me, he's a prick who likes to kill projects that existed before he did. If we can get into the competing studio before that, I think that would be smart."

"I left the competing studio head a message earlier. Dash agreed to negotiate with both studios."

He arches a brow. "You told him what's going on?"

"I did. I decided it was for the best."

"I couldn't agree more." He glances at his watch again. "We need to go," he says firmly. "If you hurry, you'll have time to change into something more comfortable, but it needs to be fast."

"Right. I'll be right down." It's a hint for him to leave while we have our clothes on and to seal that deal, I rotate and reach into my suitcase, digging for options. I remove a pair of jeans and a sweater to change into, then zip my bag. When I turn, intending to change, I run smack into Tyler's big, hard body, and drop my clothes on the ground. His hands come down on my arms, a hot branding, as he steadies me, and he says, "Easy there, sweetheart, before you take me down."

I'm fairly certain the soft, roughened-up words could be taken several ways, but all I can think of right now is his hands on my body, with the bed right behind us. He could easily maneuver me two steps, and I'd be on my back with him on top of me.

LISA RENEE JONES

CHAPTER TWENTY-SIX

Tyler

I stand in front of Bella, with the bed right behind her, and I want my hands all over her body, not her shoulders. She is so damn beautiful in ways that no other woman has ever been beautiful to me, and I can't even explain what that means. But right now, in this moment, I think of her efforts to "save" me from grief— this gorgeous woman, my employee—and I want to tell her, yes. Save me. Marry me. Or not. Fake it with me.

But I hold back.

I hold back because her being beautiful doesn't give me the right to claim her in any way. Of course, I knew she was beautiful when I hired her. I also knew she was smart and savvy in negotiations and with people. She was a win for Hawk Legal and there was never a possibility I would touch her or any other employee. *Until I did and Allison ended up dead*, I think. That was then and this is now.

It's a brutal enough thought to work me over.

I release her and step backward before she ends up on the bed, right behind her, where I want her, naked and preferably bent over that mattress. That way I can't see her gorgeous blue eyes and familiar face that remind me that she is not just some hot chick I'm banging. There is more to this than her hot body and my hard cock.

This is exactly why Bella cannot be a part of my plan to defeat my father's ridiculous marriage clause in the will. The very fact that she came to my mind before I ever left my father's attorney is unacceptable. I swore I would never touch Bella again, and that means I won't touch her again. And yet, I came to her home with the idea that she was my perfect, fake fiancée. I came to this bedroom knowing I wanted to fuck her and if she were my fiancée, fake or not, I'd have an excuse to allow myself that guilty pleasure.

I need out of this room.

"Leave your bag at the top of the stairs," I say. "I'll carry it down for you." I turn with the intent of leaving.

"Tyler."

My name on her lips is sweet bliss and brutal temptation. I want my cock between her lips, on her tongue the way she was on my tongue. I resist turning around, counting to five first, to allow my body, my cock to be specific, to calm the fuck down. It doesn't work, but I grit my teeth and turn around anyway. "Yes, Bella?"

"The suitcase is ready. I know we're in a rush and..."

I tune out the rest of the sentence, at least, for the most part, too busy thinking about kissing the words from her lips and other fantasies that involve her on her knees.

"If you don't mind?" she asks.

Fucking her before our flight? No, I do not mind at all, but that's not what she asked me. She wants me to take the suitcase with me now, not later. Perhaps she doesn't want me to have an excuse to come back to her bedroom. If she only knew how much I want to give her an excuse to keep asking me back. Holy hell.

"I got it," I say, and when I move toward her and the suitcase again, she steps aside and out of my reach, proving once again she's brains *and* beauty.

Because if she had stayed in my path, we'd both be on that bed right now. If I stay in this room much longer, we will anyway.

LISA RENEE JONES

CHAPTER TWENTY-SEVEN

Tyler

I snap up the suitcase from where it rests on the bed and it's an easy lift, too easy for as long as we're going to be gone. "We may need to be there through the weekend and into next week." I rest the case on the edge of the bed, thinking about a weekend with her, or will it be avoiding her?

"I'm prepared," she guarantees. "My clothes and shoes take up less space than yours, so it might seem like I packed less than you, but there's plenty there, I assure you. And I have another overnight bag in the bathroom. But your car isn't exactly jumbo size anyway."

"I hired a driver and we're traveling in a large SUV. Pack another bag if you need it." I walk toward the door, the exit calling to me the way a cold shower is right about now.

She surprises me then and calls out, "You really did everything possible to avoid being alone with me."

Damn it to hell, what is she doing? I pause in the doorway, reminding myself that control is golden. I don't pretend to believe she stopped me because she wants me to fuck her here and now, or anytime at all. Contrary to where my head is at, I believe Bella simply wants reassurance that all is well between us. That we can function as we once did—boss and employee—and the world will be as she knows it.

I could tell her what happened between us was a mistake. Or that I regret touching her. And I do, but not for honorable reasons. Because now I can't stop thinking about being between her legs again.

"Not enough," is my only reply before I exit the room, and I'm walking down the stairs and I don't stop there.

I exit the house into what is a chilly February late afternoon. The temperature isn't the cold shower I need right about now, but I'll take any help calming my body I can get. I walk to the rented SUV and the driver quickly accepts the suitcase. My cellphone rings and I snag it from my pocket to find my mother finally calling me back.

"Did you know?" I demand, answering the call and walking toward the porch, away from the driver.

"What did I miss?"

"Considering you're still in Europe, what haven't you missed? The *will*, Mother. Did you know the bullshit Dad put in his will?"

"Oh, good Lord. What did he do now? I feared he might pull some stunt. Judging from your tone, it didn't sit well."

She feared. Translation: she knew. Damn her. Why would I think my own mother would warn me?

A man's voice murmurs something in the background and my mother giggles like a schoolgirl. I've had enough. I hang up and text my attorney: *Any update?* and wait for a reply.

It doesn't sit well that I dropped the paperwork related to the will to him hours ago at this point. When Gavin doesn't immediately answer, I walk inside the house and find no sign of Bella, which means I'm still in wait mode. I walk to the arched doorway leading to the living room area I could merely glimpse from the entryway before now.

It's an older home, a house with a long history, every brick and board holding a story or secret about the past you may not know, but you feel its presence. If only the walls could talk and tell us what has been and should never be again. If only history didn't repeat itself, which is exactly what I do not want to happen in my life. *Allison isn't Bella*, I remind myself, but I am haunted by her death.

This old house, restored to its glory in a classic yet modern way, is what stirs these feelings, I know, and with good reason. It is much like the home my grandparents left me, where I keep my wine cellar, where Allie lived. It was part of her employment, not part of our relationship, a perk I wrote into the job description before I met her, for self-serving reasons. The wine in the cellar is safer when a staff member has it on their radar constantly.

Allie died in that house.

Ironically, so did my father.

But this house isn't that house. This is Bella's house, and it's all about classic beauty, pulled together with the façade of effortless skill. But in truth, this house's beauty was a labor of love that required hard work, skill, and dedication to achieve.

It's simple perfection. It's Bella.

"I'm ready."

At the sound of her voice, I rotate to find her standing at the bottom of the stairs in a tan sweater, matching jeans, and suede boots, a bag on her shoulder. It's not the first time I've seen Bella in casual wear. We've certainly run into each other on the weekends and a few times on the weekends at Cupcakes and Books, both of us hunting down Dash. This is, however, the first time I went from admiring how hot she is to trying to figure out how to most efficiently undress her.

It's a damn good thing we're flying commercial. If we were flying private—me and her alone—nothing good would come of it besides pleasure. Those clothes she just put on would come off at thirty thousand feet. If we made it that high with our clothes in place.

Holy hell, I need to fuck this burn for Bella out of my system with someone else that isn't her. And for the love of God, why the hell does that hold no appeal? Why can't I imagine myself making a call and flying one of the women I have an understanding with to LA? Becca would be on her knees in a heartbeat, saying, "Yes, sir" to every demand I made. But I want Bella. On her knees. On my lap. On my damn face.

"Tyler?"

At my name on her lips again—at least some part of me is—I close the space between us and reach for her bag. The act of removing it from her shoulder doesn't have to be as intimate as it becomes. My hand captures the strap and travels down her arm, and I am aware of her reaction to my touch. She draws in a breath, cuts her stare, and shivers.

Bella has not let go of what happened between us any more than I have. I slide the bag on my own shoulder, watching her closely as I ask, "Anything else?"

"Nothing," she confirms, but there is a whole lot more than nothing in the air between us.

And maybe that's the problem. There is just too much undone between us. We need it done. We need it behind us.

I drop the bag, and I'm about to just say screw making our flight, we'll fly private—and screw everything else holding me back—whatever it takes for me to get a taste of her.

CHAPTER TWENTY-EIGHT

I never get the chance to act on that thought.

My cellphone rings, almost as if my conscience is setting off an alarm. *Don't do it. Don't touch her again. Don't step back over the line.* And I don't. I grab the bag and take a step backward, placing space between me and Bella before I snake my phone from my pocket.

Gavin is on my caller ID and that is not a call I want to take in front of Bella. I decline the call. "Let's go. It's late."

"Don't you need to get that?" she asks. "I can give you privacy."

I walk to the door and open it. "Whoever it is can wait. The plane will not."

She hesitates and then grabs her long, black trench coat from the hook by the door, slips it on, and walks outside. I follow Bella to the porch, pulling the door shut. When I turn, she is there waiting on me, close, and I all but end up colliding with her again. "Bella," I chide softly.

"I have to lock up," she explains, and we're standing there again, unmoving, staring at each other. *I'm going to kiss her*, I think again.

And holy hell, my phone rings again, and I step around her and walk down the steps, removing my phone from my pocket to find my mother calling. I decline the call and pause to wait on Bella. She catches up with me. "All set?" I ask.

"Yes," she confirms. "I'm ready. What time is our flight?"

"Seven," I say, aware that it's nearing five. "We should be fine." I'm certain that we will, but we won't have time to kill time at the airport, which is fine by me. The less time I spend with Bella, the better. Or worse. It just depends on how you look at it.

The driver greets us, and I hand off Bella's smaller bag. Once he has it in hand, I open the rear door for her, and she slides inside. I join her, but she is on the other side of the car, far from my reach.

Once I've shut the door, my cellphone buzzes with a text from Gavin: *We need to talk. Call me.*

I reply with: *I'm not alone. On my way to the airport*

Good, he replies. *I hope she's pretty enough to live with. You need a fake fiancée right now. The clock is ticking on your inheritance. One you're willing to marry for at least three months. Before you object, I'm already working on a prenup that will protect you. This is a little more than one year of your life. You have to do it. Call me when you can talk.*

What about a legal challenge? Is my reply.

He has ammunition against you, Tyler. Your license and your reputation are the least of your worries. Withholding evidence is a crime. If that comes out, it will snowball. Your cases and your father's would be overturned. Suck it up and pick a bride.

My involvement in criminal law was short-lived, but my father's was not. In fact, we didn't sell off the criminal law division until two years ago, and it was long past due. It no longer fit our business model. But the selloff is irrelevant when it comes to the liability that could be created. Gavin is right. This is a problem, and I'd happily just suck it up as he demanded, but what if my father planned to use this case against me anyway? He was evil. I have to find a real answer, and marriage isn't that answer.

"Everything okay?"

At the sound of Bella's voice, I realize that the SUV is moving. I rotate to face her and she's already facing me, studying me, her blue eyes bright with worry. She could be the perfect fake fiancée. I'd come here today with that in mind. How could I not think of Bella for this role? She is gorgeous. She is intelligent. I enjoy her company. She wouldn't try to screw me in the end of all of this. But as I sit here now, facing her, I think of her job, her brother, and years of knowing each other, and 1 realize this could change her life, and affect her reputation and her career. This could become emotionally messy, even if it would be physically satisfying. We wouldn't save me from the grief I do not feel for my father or from a father with a plan to torment me right up until I inherit. All this match would do is create complications Bella doesn't need and I can't afford.

She is both the right and wrong woman for me. And yet, I speak as if she is the only woman for me, "That depends on you, Bella."

CHAPTER TWENTY-NINE

Tyler

Bella's eyes flash with a mix of emotions I cannot read, but then she doesn't force me to try, either. "Are you saying that if this film deal falls apart, I've irreparably damaged you and Hawk Legal?" she challenges. "Because that is unfair. I called you in—"

"No, Bella," I state, clearly having opened a can of worms I do not want open at all, let alone with an audience created by our driver. It was a flippant response, an almost angry reply to her concern for me after my call. A response driven by my frustration over the fake fiancée requirement and the fact that the only woman I seem to be able to think about is her.

And that is more than a small problem.

"*No, Bella*?" she asks. "What does that mean?"

"I wasn't talking about Dash's deal." I motion to the driver. "And is this a conversation you really want to have right here and now? Because I do not."

"Then what did that mean?" she counters quickly, evidently unconcerned by being overheard.

"You asked if everything was okay. I said—"

"It depends on me. The only thing that I know of that depends on me is this deal we're negotiating for Dash."

"I could have been talking about the comfort of our travels," I state rather dryly. "For instance, if you talk when I'm trying to sleep or scream with every bump on the plane."

"But you weren't saying either of those things or anything to that effect and we both know it," she counters. "Just say what you want to say to me, Tyler. I've never known you to hold back."

She has no idea how much I don't want to hold back, how much I *wouldn't* hold back if I ever had her alone, and willing, in the ways, I want her willing. But once again we have crossed a line that impacts our professional relationship and that is on me. I used her innocent question as a sounding board for too many things going on in my head. My need for a fake fiancée. My need to fuck her the hell out of my system. My concern is that will never be possible for many reasons.

And I'm agitated enough about the corner my father has shoved me into, that I don't really give two fucks right now. "You are clearly not in the same headspace as me, Bella. I thought you were better at reading me than this." I lean in closer to her. "If you were in the same headspace as me, I'm certain you'd understand the meaning. If you still do not, I'm willing to do whatever is necessary to help you understand. *When we're alone.*"

The heat of anger in her stare is replaced by the heat of understanding. "You were talking about—"

"Yes," I say because her eyes say it all. Her mind is in the bedroom, where mine hasn't left since I touched her. "I was," I add.

"Oh," she says, her cheeks flushing a warm pink.

My lips curve. "Yes, oh."

Her eyes meet mine. "I don't know what to say to that."

"Nothing. Not here. Not now." The implication is that we will talk about it later and I do believe that's what has to happen.

She scrapes her teeth on her bottom lip and turns away. I linger a moment, watching her, noting the slight tremble of her bottom lip that speaks of vulnerability and emotion. The best thing I could ever do with Bella is treat her like one of the other women in my life. To demand terms and a written agreement. I ask myself right now why I haven't considered this option.

The answer is simple. She isn't one of those other women, in every possible way. She isn't after my money or my power or even my family name. Even Allison had some of that in her, thus how she ended up with my father. Bella would hate me if I treated her as if she had one of those agendas. I'd deserve that hate, too, because I know better. And I don't want her to hate me.

Her hate is inevitable though, I realize. The minute I make the world aware of my fake fiancée, whoever she may be, Bella is lost to me. I rotate to face the front of the car and ask myself why that bothers me when it should be a relief. It will be life as usual, at least for me and Bella. She'd get over what amounts to a brief flirtation gone too far. We can get back to business. But it does bother me. Of this, there is no question.

LISA RENEE JONES

CHAPTER THIRTY

Bella

Be careful with Tyler.

The driver pulls us in front of the airport terminal and Dash's words are on replay in my head. I'm not exactly doing a fine job of heeding his warning, either. I challenged Tyler about creating a chaperoned environment for the trip and did so while he was in my bedroom. If that didn't say, *get me naked and lie on the bed with me*, I don't know what did. And that was not what I was thinking. Mostly. I thought about it, of course, I did but I was also thinking—*this is awkward.* We are so awkward, and I don't like how it feels. We will never be the same

I knew we were forbidden. As Tyler said, I knew there were consequences.

And what did I do? Moan, sigh, and orgasm, right there in his office.

All that aside, his reply when I asked him if everything was okay after he'd ended his call is driving me crazy.

That depends on you, Bella.

What the heck does that even mean?

Obviously, he'd been speaking on a personal level. He'd made that clear, but even so, he's still allowed for interpretation, and broadly, at that.

For instance: things are okay if I choose to sleep with him?

Or perhaps: things are not okay right now at all, because I can't control the obvious "hot for him" vibes I'm throwing his direction.

That second thought is jolting, and rather nauseating, too.

So much so that when Tyler opens his door on the sidewalk side of the airport, I'm not about to follow him to exit. I reach for my own door and pop the lock to crack the door. Tyler shocks me by catching my arm. "What are you doing? You're going to get hit by a car."

The only thing I'm doing right now is burning alive with his touch. "I'm fine," I say.

His eyes narrow on me and he says, "Don't run, Bella."

"I thought that's exactly what you suggested I do?"

"But I knew you wouldn't. Don't start now. Shut the door."

But he knew I wouldn't?

I've never been more confused in my life, but I do as he suggests, because exiting into traffic isn't exactly smart. I shut the door. Tyler studies me a moment, almost as if he's gauging my commitment to leaving my door shut, seconds ticking by before his hand slides away from my arm. How insane it is that I wish he'd held onto me? What is going on with me and this man?

Tyler exits the vehicle and I hesitate only a moment before I slide his direction. When I reach the edge of the high seat, Tyler offers me his hand, his eyes hooded, but I can feel his attention. This feels like a test, and I don't like tests, especially when I think I might fail. I don't enjoy that kind of negative life experience. I ignore his hand and jump out of the SUV. I don't miss the little smirk this creates on Tyler's handsome face, that *almost* reads like satisfaction, as if this is what he expected of me. What I know for sure though is that I'm not sure about anything with this man. Right now, I'm overthinking everything with Tyler.

I need to just stop with him.

That's my answer.

Stop.

I can almost hear the universe laughing at me.

LISA RENEE JONES

CHAPTER THIRTY-ONE

Bella

It's not long before we're working our way through security, and I'm being rather intimately searched by a female TSA agent while Tyler watches. His lips are curved, his eyes alight with mischief. Lord, help me, he's enjoying this. So much so that his brows go up when the lady strokes my upper leg, a bit too high and intimate.

"Ah, can we be a little more careful there, please?" I ask.

"You're done anyway," the woman replies, lifting her hand as if to say, feel free to leave.

With the hell finally over, I walk to the belt and grab my things. When I join Tyler, where he waits for me, he laughs. "That was interesting," he jokes, as we start walking toward our gate.

"For you," I say. "Not me."

He chuckles low and deep, a sexy laugh that runs a path up and down my spine, before he agrees, "I do suspect I enjoyed it far more than you."

I scowl at him, and at this point, we're walking toward our gate, and the entire act of traveling together, feels rather intimate, when it perhaps should not. But the last time I traveled with a man was two years ago, with my now-estranged almost fiancé. Travis works for the NASCAR corporate offices in Florida. We'd met at one of my father's races and instantly hit it off. He was older than me by eight years, good-looking, and well-established in life, with a dream career if you love NASCAR but don't want to drive. The age thing actually worked for us. He wasn't intimated by my career nor did he seem to see me as a payday, which is a problem when your father is famous. Actually, my brother is famous now, too. But Travis's world is my father's world.

I liked him.

My father was another story. He didn't approve. Travis just sat on the wrong side of right for him, for no named reason besides instinct, which he assures me keeps him alive all the time. I'd discounted his concern, but with a valid reason. My father has never wanted me involved with anyone in his world. Generally, his feeling is that most of them are manwhores. Probably because he's become a manwhore. But when my relationship with Travis stretched into a year-long connection, my father started to become more supportive. We even did Thanksgiving together. I thought I'd marry Travis, I really did, and so did my father. Me and Travis talked about it more and more. He broached the subject, not me, as if feeling me out for a proposal.

Then one weekend, I decided to surprise him and fly to Florida when he didn't expect me and walked into his apartment to find him with another woman. They'd been naked, in the act. At the time, I'd been devastated. My father, to his credit, never said I told you so, not once. Travis tried to win me back, but I wanted no part of it. I never even asked who she was. I didn't care. I was done. Through the process of healing, I ended up asking myself if I ever really loved him or just the idea of him. Maybe I'd loved him. I think betrayal can make you question everything about a relationship.

Tyler and I reach our gate and in doing so, I return to the present, both of us setting our things down on seats. Tyler glances at his watch. "We have more time than I thought we would. I need to make a call." He motions to the Starbucks nearby. "You want a coffee on my way back?"

"Make your call. I'll get the coffees."

"That works. I want—"

"I know what coffees you drink." I laugh nervously for pointing out my memory of all things Tyler and add, "Everyone should know what their boss likes in a cup of coffee."

He narrows his eyes on me. "Is that right?"

"Oh, yes. It's important. I take coffee and my boss's interests seriously." It's out before I can stop it, my words just tumbling into mayhem creating gibberish ever since he touched me.

Tyler's eyes light with amusement. Great. I *amuse* him. "I won't be long," he says.

"I'm really okay all by myself," I assure him.

He surprises me then and says, "Maybe I don't want you to be, Bella," and he doesn't give me time to read his words with his expression. He grabs his briefcase turns away and starts walking.

I'm left staring after him, more confused than ever. In fact, I am hereby living in a perpetual state of wanton affection and confusion where my boss is concerned. I slide my purse over my shoulder and roll my briefcase with me to the Starbucks line. I've placed the order, and I'm waiting for it when my phone buzzes with a text from Allie. *What is up with you and Tyler?*

I draw a breath and allow it to trickle from my lips. I want to tell her so many things right now. She is a friend, a sister soon, by marriage. But she also works for Tyler. She sleeps with my brother every night. There is a complicated weave to the way we are all connected.

Shouldn't you be asking about the status of Dash's Hollywood deal?

As I told Dash, you and Tyler are the dream team, but that doesn't mean I'm not worried. Him getting involved with an employee would look really bad right now. You getting involved with your boss would color the way people look at you, Bella. And I saw the way you looked at each other at the party. Y'all are red-hot together and it's terrifying me for you both.

"Anything interesting going on?"

At the sound of Tyler's voice, I rotate and face him.

"Bella, your order is ready!" comes a shout from the counter.

I hand him my phone, and say, "Read that." With that decision I can't undo, and I'm not sure I should anyway, I walk to the counter. If Allie sees what is going on between us, others will too. We have to deal with this, whatever this is, and deal with it before we return to the main offices.

I grab the drinks, return to hand him his cup, and accept my phone in exchange. "Are you going to ask why I let you read that?"

"I know why you let me read it. You're worried about your reputation at the office."

"And yours. You can't afford—"

"I know. Believe me, I know." He glances at my phone and then at me again. "Typical Allie. She tells it as it is."

"Is that how it is? I don't think we were looking at each other anyway but normal."

"When she saw us, I'd just been between your legs, Bella. Neither of us are objective on that topic."

Heat rushes to my cheeks. "Did you have to be that frank about it?"

"You had me read the message. I thought we were being frank about things?"

"We both knew what happened."

"I damn sure do," he assures me. "And she's right, Bella. We are not good for each other, but there are matters between men and women that are rarely logical."

"We can't have the world look at us and assume we're sleeping together."

A boarding announcement is called over the intercom and Tyler ignores my statement, and says, "That's us." He starts to turn away.

I don't think. I just act. I catch his arm. When his eyes meet mine the punch of awareness between us is almost brutal. "There you go touching me again, Bella," he warns softly.

I'm reminded easily of all the things he said he would do to me if I kept touching him. I release his arm. "Tyler, this is not a non-issue."

"Which is why I say we trade in these coffees for booze on the plane. We have no meetings until tomorrow. And before you say a word, your brother is wrong about alcohol being my addiction. It's not, but I am not without an addiction, Bella." His eyes drop to my mouth and linger before he looks at me with so much heat, it's hard to miss his meaning. He means me. Or sex? Sex with me? "How about that drink?" he asks.

The air crackles between us and my nipples are tingling again, and I am fairly certain I just got wet for this man, in an airport, with what might be a suggestion that I am his addiction. Or not. I don't even know for certain what he was saying.

On that note, I take his coffee from him and walk to the trashcan and throw both cups away.

LISA RENEE JONES

CHAPTER THIRTY-TWO

Bella

Turns out I'm in first class, right next to Tyler, just me and him, in a cozy nook. For this reason alone, when the flight attendant appears and before she ever speaks a word, I say, "I'll have a Bloody Mary, please."

Tyler's lips quirk with my rapid request and he orders some sort of whisky. When the flight attendant walks away, he observes. "I see you went all-in on my advice."

"Considering you offered no solution to what Allie said, and trouble is brewing, yes. I need a drink."

"Depends on how you define trouble," he replies, and the flight attendant is already back, offering us bottles to go with the glasses filled with ice. I wish she'd mix them for us. Then I could blame her for my ridiculously low tolerance for alcohol, and say she mixed it too strong.

"The good news," I say, filling my glass with a mix of vodka and tomato juice, "is that vodka all but ensures I'll sleep through the four-hour flight sitting next to you."

"I'm not sure how I feel about inspiring sleep," he replies, filing his own glass.

"You inspire a lot of things in me that are not sleep, Tyler," I assure him. "And before you run with that the wrong way, I'm in a professional headspace. There is a predominant emotion I've felt with you most of my career that is not what you will assume to insert."

"Which would be what?"

"Motivated. You're very cold about your feedback, but also honest, and usually right. I'm better for it."

"That was training. I don't remember having much feedback for you since about six months into your employment."

"I bring problems to you often, as proven by our present state of travel."

"Working together to solve a problem is not the same thing as me training you. And that's what I was doing when offering that feedback."

"In that Tyler kind of way. That's my point."

"Is this where you talk about my arrogance?" he asked.

"Which is directly related to your ego. Do we really need to talk about it?" I ask, sipping my drink. "I mean it's just so big and out there. It's not a good idea to give it more attention."

He laughs, a low, deep masculine laugh that might curl my toes if I let it, but I won't.

"You always meet me blow for blow, woman. I do like that about you. And for the record, I've never given you any suggestion you didn't beat to death."

"Hmm," is all I say, sipping again, the alcohol sending a rush of warmth over my skin. A few more sips and life will be good.

My cellphone buzzes with a message, and I quickly grab it from my purse, hoping to read the message before I get in trouble with the flight attendant. The minute I spy the number on the caller ID, I light up. "It's from Sommerby," I glance over at him, "that's—"

"The competing studio head," he supplies. "What did he say?"

"He'll see us tomorrow at nine, which is going to be rough considering it will be late when we get to our room." My eyes go wide because at this point, I'm angled toward him and somehow my leg is touching his leg. I move my leg and amend, "I mean rooms."

Tyler laughs. "You have your own room, Bella. We should talk about the strategy for the meeting though before you let that vodka put you to sleep."

I hold up a finger. "An excellent idea, boss."

His eyes darken and warm. "*Tyler*, Bella."

"I guess I could say, Mr. Hawk. Since you said Ms. Bailey the other day."

"There could be a time when that would be appropriate, Bella. You just haven't been there yet."

Suddenly, I don't know what we're talking about, but I'm pretty sure it's related to his need to dominate during sex. Which is an assumption since I haven't had sex with him, but I remember oh too well how he dominated me in his office. *Tell me what you want. Say it.*

Tyler leans in closer. "What are you thinking right now, Bella?"

"I'm not sure I moved the wash to the dryer."

He laughs again, and I don't remember him laughing in the past, as in at all, let alone the numerous times he has with me today. He's a complicated man, one with layers and layers of emotional baggage he guards well. And yet, he's let that guard down today with me.

An announcement sounds over the intercom. The short version of the message: we're taking off. I react by easing into my seat, always a bit edgy at this portion of a flight. Tyler glances over at me, those blue eyes of his seeing way too much. "Nervous flyer, are you?"

"I just don't like takeoff or landing. Those are the times you're most likely to crash. Everything in between is fine."

"You're afraid of what you can't control," he states as if it's obvious. "It's not the same way I look at control. I want it in all things. You simply dislike those things that can't be affected by anything you say or do."

It's true, of course, and I'm surprised by how well he understands my psyche even more so than my brother, and I'm close to Dash. "Per the counselor I saw at the hospital, this type of thing is normal for someone who lost a parent they were close to at a fairly young age. Though I'm not sure twenty-one is all that young."

"She died five years ago of an aneurysm, right? I believe Dash told me that, at some point."

"She was only forty-nine, with so much left to do in this world."

"The founder of the Alice Shopping Network, Alice herself. I have no doubt she did. If I remember correctly, from your job interview, you said she'd gone public and gotten out of the company?"

"Yes, she didn't like what the company looked like after the offering, but she was plotting new ways to take over the world." I tilt my head and look at him. "You didn't want to hire me because I came from money."

"I never said that."

I laugh. "You said it directly, Tyler Hawk." I deepen my voice. "*I'm going to be frank, Ms. Bailey, I don't hire people who aren't hungry. I assume you inherited a lot of money from your mother. Your father is also a rich man. It's hard to believe you could ever be what I consider hungry.*"

"Ah, that's right. To which you asked, 'Weren't you born into money and in the shadow of your successful parents? Don't you want to prove you can win because you're you?'"

"And with that, you sold me. And now, you have your success."

"I won't feel like it if this deal falls apart."

"Nothing to worry about, Bella. Per Allie, we're the dream team, remember?"

There is something in his voice, in the air between us, when he says those words. I tell myself it's all about sex. I'm in lust with him. He's in lust with me. But I've known him for years and there is a bond between us that already existed.

The plane starts to taxi at rapid speed, and I squeeze my eyes shut, feeling as if I'm about to crash and burn, and not on this plane, but with Tyler.

LISA RENEE JONES

CHAPTER THIRTY-THREE

Bella

The plane levels off and I glance over at Tyler, all comfy in his seat and sipping his drink while I'm on a proverbial ledge, about to crash.

"I guess flying doesn't bother you?"

"So much so that I got a pilot's license a few years back. Up here in the sky is the one place the rest of the world can't touch you. It's like a timeout from the chaos."

I'm not surprised he has a pilot's license. It seems like something the ultimate alpha control freak would want in his arsenal, along with a wall that is ten feet high. We hit a bump and I'm clearly on edge because I gasp. "It doesn't feel like a timeout."

His eyes brim with amusement. "It's just a little choppy air. It'll pass."

"Says the man who's a control freak. How do you not want to go check on the pilot?"

"I'm a control freak about what I can control. We're up here now. Whatever is going to happen, is going to happen. Believe it or not, flying helped me understand that there are things in life we can't change."

"Like my mother dying?" I say, slightly triggered by this topic, having far too many people in my life lecture me about my mother's death being unavoidable. And I can easily assume his trigger as well. "Or who your father is?" It's out before I can stop it. "I'm sorry. I shouldn't have said that, but I've—well, just thought of you and the struggle this must be often since he died and—"

His lips press together. "Stop trying to save me, Bella. He's gone. The end."

"Is it the end?"

He looks at me, seconds ticking by, and I can almost feel that ten-foot wall slam between us before he says, "I was talking about something more like a flock of birds flying into the engine. I can train and prepare myself for how I respond."

"Can we not talk about flocks of birds in engines right now?" I pick up my drink and down it before I say, "What does happen if a flock of birds hit the engine on a plane this size?"

"We emergency land. Did you see that movie with Tom Hanks? *Sully*? It was the true story of the pilot who landed a commercial flight in the Hudson River in New York City."

My hand goes to my neck. "Please tell me it wasn't a flock of birds?"

"It was a flock of birds that took out not one, but both engines."

I hold up a hand. "Okay, that's all I need to hear while we're in the air, thank you."

The flight attendant appears and takes our dinner orders. When she leaves, I've ordered pasta and Tyler is having fish. It's better than chicken, which is always dry and tasteless. We eat and share another drink, and end up talking through all the details of Dash's contracts, both in publishing and film. When the tables are cleared, I say, "Should we talk about the meetings tomorrow?"

"Good cop, bad cop works. We strike a deal with studio B, and make it solid. We go to studio A and I tell them to go fuck themselves, unless they meet our terms. You try to save it, tell them you're trying to get me to just go back to Nashville, but there is a lot on the line. You really want to save it, but you need a little give on their part to keep me from convincing Dash that studio B is the best choice."

"Assuming Studio B is still interested." My teeth scrape my bottom lip. "But I like where you're going with this. You're really good at taking control of situations." I tilt my head thoughtfully, thinking of all he's overcome. "Your father was a force and he tried to take control from you. He failed, Tyler. "

There's an almost angry tic to his jaw. "Are we talking about my father again?" He doesn't give me time to reply, adding, "I do like control, Bella. In all things." He doesn't give my mind time to run with the obvious implications of his words. "But maintaining control at all times can sometimes become burdensome. I require a release. I find I just need a good unattached fuck, and I'm better for it."

I blink. "I—you—"

"It works. You should try it. When you were against my office door with me between your legs, were you thinking of anything else?"

"Sex comes with complications."

"Not if you set the rules in advance. It's sex. Just sex. And nothing more."

In other words, I've been put in my place. I'm an employee. Outside of that, I was just sex to him. Because sex is just sex to him. And I am nothing to him, not on a personal level. That's what he's telling me. I crossed a line, speaking to him in a too-personal way. I can spread my legs for him, but not dare speak to him of his private matters.

The flight attendant stops by again. "Refills on your drinks?"

"Yes," Tyler says. "For both of us." He doesn't look at her. He's focused on me, a crackle in the air, a mix of sexual tension and his anger.

But not my anger.

I'm not angry. Anger will get me nowhere but embarrassed and hurt. "I'm tired. You can have my drink." I lower my seat and roll to my side, giving him my back.

CHAPTER THIRTY-FOUR

Bella

I wake to the announcement that we're preparing for landing, and find Tyler awake and working on his MacBook. The need to pee overcomes any discomfort I might feel over our earlier conflict. Him and his "I fuck" mentality did not sit well. I lay there in my seat for a good long while and replayed our conversation. With each mental repeat, my anger had stirred a bit more and blossomed into something not very pretty. He knew what he was doing when he started talking like that. He was looking for a reaction. And he got one. I shut down. Not my normal behavior, in fact, some, Tyler included, would likely call me rather dogmatic about my feelings and confrontational. But at the time we'd had the exchange, I didn't feel like pushing back really won me anything but further embarrassment. By the time I was over the embarrassment side of things, it was too late to respond differently with the same impact.

Tyler continues to click away on his MacBook as if the flight attendant has not made any announcement at all, still unaware that I'm awake. "Tyler," I say.

His head lifts, and when his eyes fall on me, there is a punch of energy between us. "Bella," he says softly, his voice gentler now, his tone almost regretful, an extreme contrast to the harshness of his mood earlier.

"We're about to land," I say. "I need to pee." He doesn't move. He just keeps staring at me and when Tyler Hawk stares at you, it feels as if he sees inside you, right to your soul. It's intense. For some, unnerving, but as he said—practice matters, and I've had plenty of practice dealing with Tyler's laser focus on me.

Well, not quite in this setting, I realize as time stretches. Truly, this is a close, intimate setting that adds a level of intensity to the moment, but then everything with Tyler is intense. This entire experience of traveling with him is unexpected. Certainly, telling my boss I need to pee, telling *Tyler Hawk* I need to pee, seems to be becoming a habit I never thought I'd form. When he still hasn't moved or said something—anything, really—I pull out my father's playbook. "If I were my father, I'd say I need to pee like a Russian racehorse."

It works. Tyler speaks, "How does a Russian racehorse pee?"

"Exactly," I say, lifting a finger. "That's what I always say. My father's reply would be *'a lot'* to which I would say *'isn't it a lot for all racehorses? They're all big.'* Then he'd say, *'you take all the fun out of jokes, Bella.'"* I firm my voice. "What I'm saying to you right now, though, Tyler, is that I need to pee like a Russian racehorse. I need you to lift your tray, please."

The flight attendant walks by and says, "Tray up, sir."

Only then does Tyler's tray go up. Now the new dilemma. Do I pass him front first or rear first? My bladder doesn't have much time for me to debate. I've been front first with him while asking him to lick certain parts of my body. I don't need a reminder. I go rear first, and I do it quickly. I hurry to the bathroom and it's a bumpy walk. The plane is jolting about, and I truly, truly have a moment, sitting on that toilet, when I think I might die like Elvis Presley. Face forward with my pants down.

I manage to get off the toilet and put myself back together. I even make it back to my row where I pause. Tyler glances up at me, expectancy in his eyes mixed with a bit of challenge. He thinks I'm afraid to walk in front of him. Well, screw him. I'm not afraid of him or anyone.

I step into our row, front first, right in front of him, and damn the plane. It jerks about and I tumble forward, right into Tyler. His hands find my waist. My hands press to his shoulders. His legs are holding onto my legs. And our eyes are locked. The punch of heat between us is combustible, the sensations rocking my body, all but orgasmic.

Still, I manage to whisper, "I'm sorry."

"I'm not," he says, and all the anger and negative energy that had been there between us vanishes, gone as if it never existed.

The plane continues to bump and jolt, and I hold on for dear life, but he holds onto me as well. A warning announcement sounds over the intercom. "Flight attendants, take your seat. Folks, this is your pilot. It's going to get a little bumpy going into LA tonight. Please stay seated and keep your seatbelts fastened."

I grab the arm of my seat and rotate into position, quickly grabbing my seatbelt and struggling with it. Tyler reaches over and helps me, his hands all over my hands. The plane suddenly drops, and I grab him and with no shame, nope, none. I bury my face in his arm. He slides his arm around me and be damned the consequences, I slide right under.

"You're a control freak," I say. "How can this not bother you?"

"I've logged a lot of air time, some good and some bad. These commercial airlines can handle a lot. I promise."

I draw in a shaky breath and nod, but I also keep holding on. If I have to dive to my death, at least I won't be alone. It's not until we're almost on the ground that the air evens out. That's when the embarrassment kicks in. I am clinging to my boss like he's the monkey bars on the playground and I want to climb him. I jerk out of his arms and flatten in my seat, scraping my teeth over my lip. I can't look at him. He made the line in the sand clear to me. Sex is sex. And I don't want to be another girl in his proverbial little black book of women. It just doesn't feel that way, but aren't the best manwhores the ones who make you feel like everything when you're with them?

"Bella," Tyler says softly.

I draw a breath and look at him. "Yes?"

"Whatever you're thinking right now, stop. This is one of those times when the ways of man and woman are complicated."

"Or not complicated at all, remember? Sex is sex. And as for stopping, I can't stop. I'm clearly not as good at the sex-is-sex thing as you are. I need us to just stop this, whatever this is. I need it to end. *Now*." As if I've timed it perfectly, the plane hits the runway. I hope the thundering sound drowns out the lies flying out of my mouth. I don't want things between me and Tyler to stop. I want them to go differently.

CHAPTER THIRTY-FIVE

Bella

Tyler and I are staring at each other when the cabin doors open and I desperately want him to say something—anything—meaningful. When he finally speaks, I get, "Damn it, Bella, what are you doing to me?"

Triggered, I twist around and poke his arm. "What are *you* doing to *me*?"

He bites out a small laugh but doesn't even try to answer my question, not that I really thought he would. "You, woman. Just you."

"You," I counter. "Just *you*."

His lips tighten. "You always have something to say."

"I didn't earlier when you were a jerk. I just went to sleep. If you'd like me to tell you what you missed because it was in my head, I can."

An elderly woman eyes us over the seat and Tyler grimaces. "I'll grab our bags."

"Young love is volatile," the woman tells me. "You'll get past it."

"Oh no," I say. "He's my boss. We're not..."

"Of course, you aren't," she says, with a smile. "Have a good night." She exits into the middle aisle.

Tyler motions for me to go ahead of him, hopefully, oblivious to the romantic advice I was just given. But we have to talk about it because this is just one more person who has assumed there is something going on between us. Once we're off the plane, we don't speak, the tension between us downright palpable. We reach baggage claim and I spot my bag, stepping forward to retrieve it. Tyler shocks me by catching my arm and maneuvering me to face him. "I'll get it."

"You don't have to—"

"I want to." He's still holding my arm. "You're right," he adds. "I was a jerk. I'm sorry."

I blanch. "Wait. Did you—just *apologize* to me?"

"I did and I meant it. I'm sorry."

I believe him and I want to ask him why he said those things to me, but there are people around us, scurrying about. This isn't the place. "Thank you for saying that," I say simply instead. "And I'm sorry, too."

"You have nothing to be sorry for. I said things I should not have and all you did was react. I'll get our bags."

He releases me and walks toward the conveyor. A pretty, dirty blonde female dressed in business attire points him out to another woman, and they tilt their heads together conspiratorially. They're talking about Tyler. Of this, I have no doubt. And how can I blame them? What a sight he is—his ass in those jeans is nothing shy of perfect. And the way he carries himself is pure dominance, with a touch of that arrogance of his that can be as irritating as it is sexy. It blasts a message that says *I can fuck you until you beg for more.* And considering my limited experience with him, I believe that's true.

Tyler retrieves my bag, and then his. He's about to return to me when one of the women—a brunette in a short skirt and heels—walks up to him and points at her suitcase, clearly asking for help. She saw him with me, but she's blatantly hitting on him. There is a distinct pinch in my chest I can only call jealousy, at least if I'm honest with myself and I try to be. Tyler walks around the luggage belt, grabs her bag, and sets it down for her. She starts talking to him, gazing up at him with lusty eyes.

Bitch.

He reaches for his phone, and my stomach knots with the idea that they're exchanging numbers. That is until I see him glance at the screen, as if he'd received a message, and hope blossoms in me that what I thought was happening is not.

He says something to the woman and then starts walking back to me, his expression focused on what is before him, not behind. He's already dismissed her. I can read this in him. He stops in front of me and says, "The driver is out front waiting on us. I don't know about you, but I'm done with airports today."

I blow off the woman, just as I believe he has. "Probably not as done as you," I say as we walk toward the door. "I slept. You didn't."

"I slept about an hour. It was enough." He opens the door for me, and I can't explain it, but there is a shift in the air between us. The tension of before has transformed into something far more old and comfortable and yet somehow, new and unknown. Even when we settle into the back of the SUV, sitting a respectable distance from each other just doesn't feel as far away as it did on the way to the airport.

It's nearly nine o'clock, which would seem to be a good time to miss traffic, but this is LA, and we end up with slow-going travel. About halfway to our final destination, the Four Seasons, Tyler's cellphone rings. He glances at his phone, a tight knot forming in his jaw as he punches in a number. "I just landed in LA. We're going to have to talk tomorrow, but tell me you have something good to tell me."

After a short pause, he says, "I think you need to open a dictionary and look up the meaning of good versus crap." Another pause and he says, "I get it. Time is ticking. I'll call you tomorrow." He hangs up and he doesn't look at me.

I'm an instinctual person, who reads people and situations well. My mother would have told you I inherited it from her. My father would say it's from him. I say it's from both. Right now, those instincts are telling me I've been drowning in hormones and missing the obvious. That shield Tyler hides behind is mighty, but it doesn't hide the truth. Tyler is not okay at all.

CHAPTER THIRTY-SIX

Bella

I draw in a breath, hyperaware of Tyler's mood on the remainder of the ride to the hotel, expecting more biting words meant to shelter him and drive me away. Almost as if he felt me getting too close, and his instinct was—is, most likely—to push me away. Because one thing I know is that Tyler's life has not been my life at all. He expects betrayal and challenges from his family, not the love and support I do with mine. He's been taught those who are closest to you can hurt you most.

Which is true. They just shouldn't.

The truth is that I'm not sure what to expect from Tyler. I'm not even sure what I want to happen. But his apology sings a new song in my mind now, the lyrics dark and tormented, written by a man battered by anger, remorse, and guilt. This is the song of a man who is haunted by demons, some of his own creation, and others by his own father. These demons hold swords meant to cut him down to a lesser being.

But as time stretches in the wake of his phone call, I sense none of what I anticipated in Tyler at all. We finally bypass the traffic and arrive at the Four Seasons after ten o'clock. The driver pulls us to the front door of the hotel, and an employee opens Tyler's door, but not mine. This time when Tyler exits the vehicle, I follow and when he offers me his hand again, and my eyes meet his, it's as if a magnetic force as alpha and demanding as Tyler himself, drags us together. It's a force I cannot resist and therefore there is no hesitation in me. I press my hand to his, warm all over with his touch, with the intimacy of the moment. His large fingers close around mine, and he holds onto me, walking me to him. When I'm in front of him, close enough to lean into him but far enough that our bodies do not touch outside of our hand, he tilts his head down, inhaling as if he just wants to breathe me in.

A shiver races up my spine, and I can feel him in every part of me. "Bella," he says softly, "you need to know—"

"Your tickets for your bags," the doorman offers, cutting off what he might have said.

I am left hanging on a limb, waiting for what feels like a confession, or maybe it's simply a warning about him and sex for sex. I can't know. Tyler releases me and turns to the other man. "We only have a few bags. I've got them." He palms the man a tip.

I grab my purse and roller bag, but Tyler claims my larger bag as well as his own items, maneuvering the load toward the door and then into the lobby. "I'll check us in," he says, indicating a couch. "You wait."

I nod because I can't seem to find my voice. It, and every part of my body, is presently being ravished by a wild and wicked mix of nerves and lust for Tyler Hawk. *But I'm not going to sleep with him*, I tell myself. It doesn't matter that the heat is burning us alive. I have to think about the damage to our work relationship. His sex-is-sex motto works for him, but it's never going to work for me. Of course, everything about me and relationships is confusing right now. I want one, but I don't believe in love. So, what is it that I really want? Do I even know?

Tyler Hawk.

I want him.

In a futile effort to distract my mind from *my boss*—and he *is* my boss—I glance around the hotel, with all its glitz and glamour, but I'm unaffected. I mean, yes, it's gloriously decorated, and the hotel is favored by talent and executives for business meetings, but I've seen it all before. I'm also not impressed by Hollywood in general, but then it's not all that unfamiliar to me. Not only is Nashville its own version of Hollywood, but I also grew up in the world of NASCAR, and cameras and my father's fans were just always a part of our world. I'm comfortable around fame. And being comfortable in this world has served me well. I'm not asking for an autograph, but rather a signature on the dotted line.

Tyler finishes up at the registration desk and joins me, offering me a room key. "You're all set. Go get some rest. I'm going to grab a drink and then do the same."

It's a dismissal, but it doesn't read like what he really wants, though I don't know what to say either. "Okay," I say. "Goodnight." *This is the right decision*, I tell myself. It's the *right decision*. I grab my bag and turn away from him, walking toward the elevator. Oh God, I want him to follow, and I can feel his eyes on me, but not the warmth of his body. There is emptiness in my wake. He's not following me.

With a lurch of my stomach, I reach the elevator bank and punch the button, but I don't look in Tyler's direction. I don't want to know that he's not there. The doors open and I step inside. It's a fast, lonely ride, and when I reach my floor, I hurry to my room in desperate need of a private place to gather my emotions. I unlock the door and step inside to what is a stunning suite, and not one of the lower-end ones. Tyler gave me what has to be a next-level Presidential Suite. So what room is he in?

The bar, drinking, I think.

That's okay. Dash is worried about his drinking. It's not the answer.

I don't give myself time to talk myself out of my next move. I unload all of my stuff, even my purse, and exit my suite. I'm going to find Tyler.

CHAPTER THIRTY-SEVEN

Tyler

What the hell is Bella doing to me? I have never wanted a woman more than I want her and yet I just walked away. Because I'm trying to do right by her.

I enter the bar and eye the clusterfuck of random leather booths and wooden tables. I have no idea why Hollywood favors this place. Everything is too close together for privacy and forces an intimacy that I for one, don't want when I'm in hardcore negotiations. Tonight though, the place is dead, and I slide into a booth with an empty chair across from me.

The pretty blonde waitress is quick to appear by my table and I decide it's an expensive whiskey kind of night. "Macallan 25. Just bring the bottle and no, I don't care how much it costs."

"No problem, sir," she says, smiling a flirty little smile. "Coming right up." She sashays away and I don't give her another look. There is only one woman on my mind right now, or at any time as of late. The honest-to-God truth of the matter is I always had a thing for Bella, which is why I was careful with her. It's why I always made sure I traveled separately from her, but not this time. I knew the dangers of us being together and I convinced myself commercial travel was all the barrier we needed between us.

The waitress sets the bottle on the table. "I didn't know if you wanted ice or no ice, so I brought you two glasses. I can pour for you."

"I got it. Thanks." I dismiss her because I need to be clear. No is the answer. Sure, I could take her to my room and fuck her blind, but I'd be thinking about Bella.

She walks away and I fill a glass, thinking about the call I'd had with Gavin. I'm going to have to pick a woman and wear her on my arm for the better part of a year. Hell, I may have to marry her. I pull up my phonebook and start scanning the names. I don't even know if I like any of these women. I don't spend that kind of time with any of them.

My cellphone rings and I retrieve it from my pocket to find Gavin on my caller ID again. "I hope this call has some fucking good news," I answer.

"Can you talk?"

"Yeah," I say, sipping from my glass, because I'm going to need the booze to handle this conversation. "I'm alone."

"The only way you get out of this is going to court," he states. "How impossible is that?"

"You read my father's note. I go to court, and he ruins me and the firm. Everything I have lived for my entire life is ruined."

"I read the case file your father used to threaten you. What's the story?'

"My father withheld evidence and told me the clients threatened to kill us if he didn't do it. Which, knowing what I know about the family in question, I believe."

"Who's the family?"

"The Allen family."

"As in the family that owns half the state of Tennessee?"

"That would be them."

He whistles. "Okay, well, that's some power. I think you're fucked. Do you have a woman in mind, because, man, I think you are going to have to marry her. Make sure you can tolerate her for at least nine months—six engaged and three married—which is the timeline your father set for a public display, and then give me a chance to have her checked out."

There is only one woman I can more than tolerate. *Bella*, I think, but Dash would kill me, and I'd ruin her reputation. "I'll get you a list. The one that checks out as the least likely to fuck me, and most likely to make my staff and clients feel secure is what matters."

"Sorry, man. I'm going to continue to look for loopholes. I'll draft the contracts for your "fake fiancée/bride" as well, for you to review. And the sooner you get the six months started, the sooner it's over.

We disconnect and I down my drink.

If I don't go upstairs and knock on Bella's door now, while she will still open the door for me, I'll never get another chance with her. Sweet, sexy, incredible Bella, who tastes like honey, and goes to war with me like a UFC fighter, all-in, and swinging. I want to go to her. It's the wrong decision, I remind myself, and refill my glass. I have until this glass is empty to convince myself that's still a bad decision. And it's going to be a hard sell.

LISA RENEE JONES

CHAPTER THIRTY-EIGHT

Bella

I cannot believe I'm doing this. He sent me to my room. He basically rejected me, and what am I doing? Hunting him down, which is craziness, but apparently, I'm highly committed to this decision because my feet just keep on walking.

With nerves tap dancing in my belly, I step into the entryway of the bar and my eyes cut through the dim lighting to land on Tyler, sitting at a table and nursing a half-filled glass. My heart races and my body is in overdrive, shooting hormones left and right but with good reason. Tyler Hawk sits at a table like he's a king. He owns the bar. I'm fairly certain he owns my body, which probably means I should have stayed in my room, but that ship has sailed.

At present, his gaze is fixed on his phone as if he's reading a message, and I take advantage of his distraction. With a deep breath, I close the space between me and him and I've slid into the seat in front of him before he ever knows I'm present.

His gaze lifts, eyes darkening, his reaction to my presence unreadable in their depths as he says, *"Bella."*

There is something utterly arousing about how he says my name, as if he's breathing me in with a word. But maybe that's what I want to be happening. Maybe it's more utter frustration that he can't get rid of me. He sets his phone down on the table, "What are you doing here?" he asks, which only serves to stir an extra special dose of insecurity that settles hard in my already nervous belly.

I set my room key on the table. "You gave me the wrong room. I thought I could exchange the key and leave you this one. I'll get my stuff out and—"

"It's your room, Bella. I wanted you to have it."

"Why would you give me the better of the two rooms? You're the boss."

"Because you deserve it."

I wet my lips and there is no missing the way his eyes follow my tongue. I suck in a breath and fight the urge to fold my arms in front of me to ease the ache of my nipples. Instead, I settle them on the table and lean in close, and the choice of room is the last thing on my mind.

"Talk to me. As a friend, not an employee."

"Some would say you can't be both," he replies. "I'm your friend, Bella. Screw *some,* whoever they are."

He strokes his jaw, and I can't help but notice his hands, his long fingers. I can't help but think about them on my body. I force myself to focus on what is important. He is important. "Talk to me," I urge again.

"I was just thinking about my father."

"What about him?"

"He was a bastard to me, but I learned a lot of useful things from him. It's hard to reconcile that the man who built a billion-dollar empire and held me to the standards he did, and the one who took an innocent life."

I'm shocked at his openness, but also twisted in knots. He's thinking about Allison, not me, and how horrible is it of me to even have these thoughts about him when he's grieving? I'm a horrible person. "Did you love her?"

His eyes sharpen and so does his voice. "Asked and answered. I didn't love her, Bella, but that makes me feel like a real prick. I still have her journal. I can't bring myself to even read the damn thing. It's all about me. It's a hard viewpoint to swallow."

The waitress appears and gives me a once over I don't really understand. "A drink?" she asks, and it hits me then that she had her sights set on Tyler. I don't like it. Not one bit.

I eye Tyler's bottle of whiskey, Macallan 25, an insanely expensive bottle. "I'll have some of his," I say and reach across the table, taking the glass right out of his hand, and sipping the smooth-as-silk whiskey.

When I'm done, the waitress is gone. Tyler's lips quirk. "That's the way to get rid of her."

"I wasn't getting rid of her, but I've never actually tried the 25. It's amazing."

"So you thought you'd just have a sip from my glass?"

"Is that a problem?" I challenge.

He eases forward, closing much of the space between us. "No, Bella. It's not a problem. Friends tonight, right?"

"If that's true, why were you down here drinking alone?"

He studies me a moment and eases back in his seat, almost as if I've reminded him why talking to me is a bad idea. "I was trying to protect you."

"From what? You?"

"Yes. From me."

"We've covered this. I don't need protection. Tell me what's going on with you, Tyler. Use tonight to actually talk to someone who you can trust. And you can trust me."

"I know I can trust you."

"Then what's the problem?"

"It's not appropriate to talk to you about this," he says.

"Not appropriate? I think that ship has sailed with us."

He downs the contents of his glass and refills it. I take the glass right out of his hand again. It's mine now. "Use me, not the bottle."

"Use you." He laughs a bitter laugh. "You have no idea what a loaded offer that is, Bella."

"I am many things, but naïve is not one of them."

"You'll just end up hating me and I really don't want you to hate me. I'm actually surprised by just *how much* I don't want you to hate me, Bella."

He's confusing me again, sending mixed messages. "I'm not as delicate as you think."

"I have never thought of you as delicate except when you were on my tongue, woman, and that was the right kind of delicate. You're special, Bella. Sweet like honey and pure fire at the same time."

I swallow hard with the surprisingly intimate and wildly erotic words he's spoken, and there is no escaping a memory of him on his knees, licking my clit while I moaned. But I shove it aside with rough insistence, all too aware of what he's doing. "You can't shock me into seeing nothing but sex, Tyler. Because sex is clearly how you solve problems. But *this* is how easily I shock. This isn't about how I taste on your tongue. It's about something else. What is that something else?"

CHAPTER THIRTY-NINE

Bella

Seconds tick, his words and my words, the memory of our intimacy hanging in the air between us before he laughs one of his deep, wonderful laughs, and says, "God, woman. You're really everything I don't expect."

"Is that good or bad?"

"To be decided. My mother is in Europe," he adds, in what is a seemingly random reply.

I blink in confusion but follow the lead he's given me. "Again?"

"Still. She ran off with a man and hasn't been back. I don't know if she's coming back."

"Is that causing a complication for Hawk Legal?"

"No. She's completely out of the picture, per my father's will. From what I've put together, by the numbers, she got half his wealth and none of his hell. Apparently, she knew a long time ago but didn't tell me."

"What does that mean, she's known for some time and didn't tell you?"

"My portion of the will wasn't read until this week."

"Why the delay?"

"It's all part of a head game my father is playing."

"As in via his will."

"Exactly," he confirms.

"What does that mean?"

"He placed stipulations to my inheritance that impact the stability of the company, therefore the security of the staff. If I don't do what he demands, not only will I not inherit, but I'll also lose my stock. That would force the firm's leadership into limbo, and the operation into chaos."

"Oh my God," I breathe out. "Based on your mood, I'm afraid to ask but I have to. What are the stipulations?"

"You *don't* want to know, Bella."

My heart thunders in my chest for not a good reason, as if what he has to say is about me when that's not even slightly possible. "Tell me."

"Take a drink first."

I sip long and deep, and he motions for me to hand him the glass. I don't argue. I slide the glass his direction. He picks up the bottle and refills it, downing everything he's poured before he says, "I have to marry within fifteen months, but first, I have to put on a show with my *fiancée* for at least six months. My womanizer father wants me to marry for the good of the company."

I can barely breathe, as in literally my lungs don't want to draw in air for a full three seconds. My heart is now beating at a rate that I'm fairly certain means I'm screaming inside. "Is there a way out of it?" I hear myself ask, but my voice sounds hollow and distant.

"No," he says, his expression stark. "He did something dirty with one of his cases years ago. I was co-counsel and therefore attached. If I fight the will, he arranged to make that public, which would get me disbarred and every case my father or I touched would be challenged. It would ruin the company. People will lose jobs. I'm the prisoner of a dead man."

"There has to be a way out of this."

"Of course, I'm looking at options, but for now, I have to move forward as if this is irreparable."

"This is insane, Tyler. I mean, what next? You interview potential fiancées?"

"My attorney wants me to send him a list of potential candidates. He'll check them out, pick one, and we'll create a contract. Not long after the wedding, we'll divorce." He lifts the bottle. "Now you see why I'm drinking."

This isn't what I expected him to say. He's just accepted this. He's doing it. "This is crazy." My voice trembles and a wave of just as crazy emotion washes over me. Emotion that feels like pain, hurt. I feel betrayed. I feel cheated on, which is illogical. He's my boss, not my boyfriend. Certainly not my fiancé.

I lift his glass and down the contents, choking a bit with the volume of the liquid. "I need to go." I try to stand up.

Tyler captures my hand, and I hate the tingles that run up my arm. "Bella—"

"Please, let go of me. I know you don't understand how I feel right now because I don't either, but I'm upset. I have no right to be upset but I can't change the fact that I am. Upset. Very upset. I just...I need space. I need to go to bed and sleep and I'll be me again tomorrow."

"Don't do this."

"What is it I'm doing, Tyler, besides what you tried to do when you sent me to my room? I'm sparing us both a complication we don't need."

"I didn't plan on whatever this is between us any more than I want to be in this position. Jobs and lives will be affected if I don't do this."

"You owe me no explanation."

The waitress reappears by our table. "How are we doing over here?"

I grimace at her attention that's meant for Tyler. "Maybe she can go on the list," I suggest, and I jerk my hand from his. The minute I'm free, I slide out of the seat, snatch up my room key, and rush away. "Bella!" I hear Tyler call out, but I don't look back.

He has a several thousand-dollar tab and a waitress to interview. He doesn't need me.

I manage to make it into an elevator without falling apart. Once inside the empty car, my hand trembles but I swipe the keypad and punch in my floor. I hug myself and rock. He's getting married. He's going to be engaged any minute now to someone he used as a sex toy. Why do I even care? He's a man with a list of women to fit this agenda. What does that say about him?

The elevator halts and the doors open. I all but fly out into the hallway. My God, I think I might have real feelings for Tyler. My eyes burn and I'm fighting back tears. I'm falling apart. I'm emotionally invested in Tyler, and I didn't even see it happening. Maybe I have been for longer than I want to admit. Lord knows we had plenty of one-on-one meetings and dinners with clients. We are not new to each other.

My key isn't opening the door. I press my hands to my face. I can't go back down there right now. I can't see him right now.

"Bella."

My heart lurches at the sound of his voice and my name. I turn to find Tyler striding toward me and I can barely breathe all over again. *What is he doing*? "What are you doing, Tyler?"

By the time I've asked the question, he's in front of me, dragging me to him, his powerful legs framing my legs, his fingers tangling into my hair. "This," he murmurs, and then his mouth comes down on my mouth, and he's kissing the hell out of me, right here in the hallway.

CHAPTER FORTY

Bella

Tyler ravishes my mouth with his mouth, and any resistance I might muster up on behalf of my aching heart simply evaporates. If I had even one little bit of self-preservation left, I'd push him away and send him back to his list of prospective fiancées. But this is a fleeting thought, drowned out by the intoxicating taste of him, and the feel of his hard body pressing me against the door, caging me as if he assumes I will run.

I counter that assumption with my hands, running them up his back and folding myself into him, my breasts pressed to the solid wall of his chest, nipples puckered in tight little balls beneath the lace of my bra. My message, I hope, is clear. I don't need to be convinced to stay one little bit. He seems to read me, and he doesn't require additional encouragement. He reaches for my arm and drags it to my side, his hand catching mine, retrieving the key I'm still holding. Without a word, he swipes it across the keypad. The light turns green for him immediately, with no resistance at all, almost as if I was meant to wait in that hallway for him to find me.

"You're going to have to share your room with me, sweetheart," he says, and he doesn't allow me time to object or even savor that endearment, not that objection is on my mind. I'm thinking of nothing but his mouth and hands on my body and this time, *mine on his.*

He opens the door and enters the room, maneuvering me along with him. The door slams shut behind us, and he's already kissing me again. This time when his fingers find my hair, he gives the long strands an erotic tug and drags my gaze to his. "Control in all things, Bella. It's who I am. It's what I need, not a want."

"And as you remember," I say, my fingers curling on his chest, "I don't like what I can't control, which I guess actually means I like control, too."

"And you have it with me," he promises. "Always. All you have to say is no, and we find what feels like a yes to you. You asked if I trust you. I'm asking you now if you trust me."

I consider the complexity of the question. Do I trust him to listen when I say no? Yes. Do I trust him not to break my heart? I'm pretty sure that's signed, sealed, and delivered, so, no. Do I trust him to make tonight all about pleasure? The kind of pleasure I'll remember long after he is married off to his future fiancée. Yes. That's a brutal yes because of where this is headed, which is nowhere but right here, right now, but one I can't walk away from, either. "Yes," I say. "I trust you."

"I don't think you do, *Bella*," he murmurs, and the way he uses my name—it's as if he wants me to know I'm not just sex to him. Or maybe I just want to believe that—even *need* to believe that—to be here with him, to be this intimate with him. Because I'm still me. I'm still not the sex-is-sex kind of girl, even if he aspires to change that in me. "But I want you to trust me so damn badly it's insane," he adds roughly, an edge of frustration in him, as if this statement somehow contradicts the control he so values.

It shakes me just how much I'm pleased that I've tormented him in some way, as if it's selfish of me. I know this, but Lord also knows I'm tormented over this marriage agreement he's obviously accepted. And if I think too hard about it, I will run. I will leave.

I don't want to leave.

I press to my toes, desperate for his mouth and body, for that oblivion he's shown me once that I crave again.

His grip tightens gently around my hair, the act both arousing and brutal, as he denies me his mouth. "I'm going to make you trust me, Bella," he declares, and then, thank you Lord, his mouth slants over my mouth, his tongue caressing my tongue. And it's a toe-curling, deep, drugging kiss that leaves me breathless when his lips part mine. "Get undressed," he orders. "I want to watch." He releases me and I am instantly cold where I was hot only moments before.

I stand there in disbelief as he sits down on the end of the bed, and I'm left standing, stunned by this sudden turn of events, by the way this has become the Bella show. It's not like I'm inexperienced in the bedroom. I've certainly been treated like a Stretch Armstrong doll many a times by Travis. It often felt as if I was a toy he played with, not a woman he was making love to. I feel as if this should feel the same, but it doesn't. I feel vulnerable, and wildly aroused, but also intimidated by the idea of standing naked in front of Tyler Hawk when he remains fully dressed. And yet, the burn of anticipation is as present as anything I've ever felt in my life.

"Undress, baby," he says, that endearment, spoken softly, is the undoing of me, while the idea of being on show and at his mercy is also surprisingly arousing. And yet I hesitate, nervous energy, zipping wildly through my body.

Tyler reads me all too well, pushing to his feet and erasing the space between us in a few short steps. His hands settle under my hair on my neck, and he tilts my gaze to his. "Just be in the moment, Bella," he urges gently. "Don't overthink everything."

"Why can't you just do what you're doing now? Touch me."

"It's better when you want and wait until you can want and wait no more."

"I think we've had plenty of time to want and wait, Tyler."

"And not enough time to enjoy being here, baby. I want to savor every minute with you and every inch of you."

Heat settles low in my belly and my sex clenches, fingers curling around the cloth of his shirt. "It's hard. We are—"

"Hot as hell for each other and that feels really damn good. I'm where I want to be right now. Are you?"

Right now.

I hate that I focus on the "right now" as a negative, a reminder that I'm nothing to him in the big picture. A reminder too, that sex is sex for him. But "right now" is also all that I'll ever have with him and I'm not sure I will ever be as sexually charged with anyone else in this lifetime. I mean, if I don't believe in love anymore, why am I denying myself pleasure? I'm *not* going to deny myself pleasure. He's right. It's time to stop overthinking.

"Yes," I say. "Yes, I am right where I want to be."

He brushes his lips over mine, his teeth nipping my bottom lip before he says, "I own you tonight, Bella. You're mine. Say it. You know I'm going to make you say it."

My lips curve and I don't know what he expects of me, but it won't be easy submission. He'll have to work for it. "Yes," I say. "I know what you want, but as for owning me, even for tonight. You can try."

LISA RENEE JONES

CHAPTER FORTY-ONE

Tyler

I stroke my thumb over her cheek and say, "Challenge accepted, baby. Now you're going to undress for me."

"And if I don't?"

"Then I'll bend you over and fuck you and then it's just over. And it would be a damn shame to waste this pent-up fuck energy on a quickie, don't you think?"

She scrapes her teeth on her lip, a nervous energy to the action as she asks, "And if I undress for you?"

"Then we fuck properly, with our mouths and hands first, all over each other." I scoop her backside and mold her hips to my hips. The thick bulge of my erection presses to her belly, while my cheek presses to her cheek. "I'll finger fuck you and tongue fuck you until you can't take it anymore. But I won't let you come. That way, when I slide my cock inside you, Bella, you'll be so tight and wet for me, you'll buck against me and beg for more. You'll get me so hot that I'll be fast, and we'll have to do it all over again. The next time, nice and slow."

Her nails dig into my shoulders, and she pants out a breathy, "Tyler," which is one step closer to "*Please, Tyler*." *We'll get there*, I think. We will most definitely get there. I cup her face and force her gaze to mine, a mix of vulnerability and challenge in her eyes I find sexy as hell. "I feel like I've wanted to be inside you for a lifetime, Bella. And now I wait for your decision. Undress or—"

"Undress," she says, wetting her lips and pushing out of my grip. "I'll undress, but you just made a lot of promises you have to keep."

My lips quirk with her fiery reply, but I can feel the nervous energy wafting off her. I decide her ex, Travis, who I've met and disliked, obviously didn't know how to take care of his woman. She is too confident and secure in herself to be this resistant to good sex. Either something happened to her, or she's just plain had bad lovers who didn't pay attention to what she was telling them. I won't make the same mistake.

And what she needs is for me to slowly earn her trust and learn her body, and that means time. I'll never get that with her. She'll never touch me again after I pick this ridiculous, fake fiancée. I have tonight with her, and I plan to make it count. I close the space between us and catch her hip. Her eyes warm with the action, and she says, "What are you doing? I thought—"

"Take off your boots, baby." It's the least intimidating command I can give her.

She searches my face, looking for an explanation for this turn of events, and I don't know what she finds, but I hope it's a man who never wants to hurt her but knows he will. I can't stop it from happening. It's too late. Whatever she sees in me, for once, she obeys. She grabs my arm and uses me for the stability I intended as she tugs one boot and then the other off and tosses them aside. "You're shorter than I thought you were."

She laughs. "Five-four isn't short. You're just tall."

"Six-three," I say, tenderness I am not accustomed to feeling rushing over me as I stroke her hair behind her ear, and I don't miss the way she shivers in response. There is something about this woman. Something unfamiliar and addictive.

"As big as your ego," she teases.

"I should have seen that one coming," I say, aware of the new territory I am in. I told her I fuck away my problems. And I do. I just fuck. I don't talk. I didn't even talk to Allison, but I'd tired of the revolving door. I'd just fuck. This is not the right headspace. Or maybe it is. This is getting too personal. This is one night. That's all it can be.

I catch Bella's hip again and drag her against me, cupping her head. "It's been too long since I kissed you. My mouth slants over her mouth and kisses the fuck out of her, and holy hell, I want to drown in everything that is this woman. My hands are all over her, and I want to be buried so deep in her, I'll never find a way out.

I catch the hem of her sweater, and her hand captures mine. "I thought you wanted me to undress for you. You're not getting away with that fast fuck and it's over. You made a promise." Her eyes are brimming with mischief and that confident side of her I know well has settled back into place.

Because it became about me and her, and whatever this connection we have is not just sex.

Damn it. I am getting this all wrong, but I don't seem to want to be right because I want everything I don't deserve with her. I sit down on the bed and Bella starts to undress. And it wouldn't matter if the ground shook with an earthquake or if the biggest client at Hawk Legal called me right now. Nothing is taking me away from Bella.

LISA RENEE JONES

CHAPTER FORTY-TWO

Tyler

Her silky blonde hair drapes over her breasts, nipples puckered and rosy. Her hips curvy and her belly tight. If I had to describe my perfect woman, it would be Bella Bailey. And she stands in front of me naked and willingly vulnerable.

"Now what?" she asks, her eyes meeting mine, a playful challenge in their depths.

Now what, indeed? I don't know why she was hesitant earlier, but she is fiery now. I push to my feet and walk to her, stopping close, but not too close. She reaches for me, and I catch her hand. "Don't touch me until I tell you to touch me."

"Why?"

"Because I said so. No other reason. I touch you. You don't touch me."

"But I *want* to touch you. I waited a long time."

"How long, Bella?"

Her chin and lashes lower. I place a finger under her chin and ask, "*How long?*"

"Too long."

I walk behind her and when she tries to turn, I catch her waist. "I said, don't move. And, yes, baby, it was way too long to get here." I slide my hand around her to her belly. "There are so many things I want to do to you and with you. I don't even know where to start." I press a hand to her backside. "Have you ever been spanked, Bella?"

"No!" She tries to turn. "And no."

"Easy, baby," I murmur, close to her ear, anchoring her to me. "No is no. I knew that would be your answer. I wanted you to know I'm okay with that." I begin caressing her body all over, her backside, her belly, her sex, over and over again. "But it can be incredible. You across my lap. Me stroking you between your legs, preparing you. And, oh God, baby, when it's done and I'm inside you, it's an orgasm you will never believe." My fingers slide down the crevice of her backside, to her sex.

"Tyler," she pants.

I move her near the desk and press her hands to the wood, "What are you doing?" she asks anxiously, eyeing me over her shoulder.

"Admiring your beautiful ass." I stroke her between her legs, my fingers sliding inside her in a quick tease that has her arching into the touch. Once I know she's lost in the sensation, I squeeze her cheek before I give it a tiny smack.

She yelps and rotates to face me, her breasts all bountiful as she confronts me, grasping the desk on either side of her. "What was that?" she demands.

I pull her into my arms. "A love pat, baby. Just a love pat." I kiss her hard and fast, and she tangles her fingers into my hair, giving it a rough tug.

"You're brutal."

"Hmmm. And you like it, baby. You know you do."

"Too much," she whispers, and there's a shift in the air, an emotional bomb that just landed right there between us, dropped by the heavens above I swear, because I didn't do it. And I don't even think she did.

"Now it's my turn to order you around," she says. "Get undressed."

"Only if I can spank you," I say.

"Not this time," she whispers, her fingers stroking the stubble on my jaw.

"That's not a no."

"It's not a yes."

"I can live with a maybe," I say, and I step back from her, and pull my shirt over my head.

She smiles at what she sees and says, "Now I can watch you."

I laugh. "Yes. Now you can watch me."

When I have put on my show for her and I'm naked, my cock jutting forward so freaking hard it hurts, she eyes me and licks her lips. "You'll pay for that," I promise her. "Because I haven't even gotten started with you tonight." I hold up the condom in my hand. "Come put it on for me."

She pushes off the desk and does as I've ordered, stopping in front of me and taking the condom in one hand and my cock in the other. "You don't need this. I'm still on the pill and if you give me something, I know where you live and work. I will come at you, no matter who your fiancée is." She tosses the condom.

The words punch through the air and slam into me. "Bella," I say and reach for her, but my damn cock is between us and still in her hand.

She presses on my chest and swallows hard, her eyes tormented though I'm not sure if she knows how transparent she is because she says, "It was a bad joke. And I know what you really want. Me on my knees." And that's exactly what she does. She goes down on her knees and licks my cock.

It's a damn unfair way to win a war of words.

LISA RENEE JONES

CHAPTER FORTY-THREE

Tyler

Bella on her knees with my cock in her mouth is a fantasy come to life. It was my intent to talk to her about this bullshit my father has created for me and now us, but holy hell, her tongue. She's licking me like I'm a damn lollipop, which is exactly how my fantasy played out. It's almost like she's in my head, when I'm the one who needs to be inside her. Because if she keeps this up, I'm going to unload in her mouth and ruin the hell out of this night.

She sucks me deep and I groan, low and rough. I reach for her and my fingers twine in her hair, guiding her to keep going. But that's not what's in my head—the one that actually thinks and makes proper decisions—the one telling me that I'm screwing this up with Bella. I'm being selfish, allowing my pleasure to be the priority. She won't remember my pleasure tomorrow. She'll remember hers and I want her to remember. That's it. We're done, at least with this. I catch her arms and with supreme effort, drag her away from my cock.

Confusion etches her beautiful features. "You didn't like it?"

I stroke her hair and say "Baby, it was a perfect fantasy come to life, and yes, I've had that fantasy, and about you. But this is not how I want tonight to end." I scoop her up and carry her to the foot of the bed where I set her on her feet again. I sit down, frame her hips, and walk her close, between my legs. My hands caress up her backside and I kiss her belly. Her body trembles in response.

She bites her bottom lip and dives her fingers into my hair and she stares down at me with heavy-lidded eyes. "You had fantasies about me?"

"Yeah, baby, I did. I was never going to act on them, but then you came to my apartment and seduced me with *Dirty Dancing*."

She smiles, and says, "Swayze had a way about him," only to pant and bite her lip, as my fingers slide along her slick sex. "God, you're so damn wet," I murmur, slipping a finger in and out of her, my opposite hand stroking over her breast, fingers tweaking her nipple.

Her hands come down on my face and she leans in and presses her forehead to mine. "I don't want to come like this either, and if you don't stop, I will. Can you just be inside me now, already? *Please,* Tyler."

And there is the word I most wanted from her, because they tell me she's all in, one hundred percent present and accounted for. I cup her head and kiss her, scooping her backside as I do and then leaning in to kiss her clit. "Tyler," she breathes out desperately. "I'm about one right move from coming. Please, *please* be inside me when that happens."

I pull her onto my lap. She eagerly climbs on board, her hands settling on my shoulders, her amazing breasts between us, right at my mouth's reach. I capture her waist, anchoring her, kissing one stiff peak, even as she wraps her hand around my cock and guides me where she wants me. She presses my throbbing erection inside her, and she is tight and wet, and it's about the closest thing to heaven on Earth I can imagine.

When she has all of me, her hands press to my face, and she leans in, her lips above mine as she says, "I'm not going to regret this. How could I?"

That brings me back to Earth with a crash. *Too easily,* I think, but she's caught in the moment. Right here, right now, she believes tomorrow will be sunshine and daisies while I know differently. For that reason, the sincerity of her words, her belief, cuts me like a knife. I drag her mouth to mine, kissing her with the fierceness of a man who wants to own the woman he's inside. Our bodies start to sway together, and I cover her breasts with my hands, and she covers my hands with her hands. She eases back, squeezing my shaft, her eyes meeting mine as she rides me, and rocks against me.

I lean down and suckle her nipple. Her hands are back in my hair, but I fold her into me, her breasts to my chest, and we're swaying, wild, fast, and then nice and slow. Our breath mingles together, our lips close, and then we're kissing again, touching each other, and I swear to God, when I bury my face in her neck, I want to inhale her, and consume all that she is. I roll her to her back and settle on top of her, her legs spread, one lifting to my hip. I catch her knees and pull them to her chest, and thrust into her, and I'm still not deep enough. I shift both of her knees to my chest, cup her backside and curl her into me, rocking with her. She grabs my shoulders, or tries, and her eyes squeeze shut, sounds of pleasure, hers and mine, filling the air.

I can feel the squeeze of her sex around me, feel how close she is to tumbling over the edge. I roll off with her, taking her with me, and us to our sides, pulling her leg to my hip, shifting our bodies until we're nice and snug. "Good?" I ask softly.

Her fingers curl on my cheek and she says, "Perfect."

There is no better word for a man inside a woman, and my mouth crashes down on hers, my tongue and cock stroking deep. She presses into me, and I mold her close, urgency building between us again, expanding, and then exploding into release. She trembles in my arms and I quake in response. When we're done, we collapse into each other. For long seconds that stretch into a full minute, we just lay there, our bodies entwined.

I finally force myself to reach behind me and grab the box of tissues on the nightstand, pulling out tissues and handing them to her. "Thanks," she says, and then, "I should go to the bathroom." Just like that, she is rolling off the other side of the bed and grabbing her clothes as she races to the other room. The door shuts with a thud. I sit up and run my hand through my hair. Already she's regretting this. I stand up, grab my pants and pull them on and then stand outside the door.

I knock. "Bella?"

She opens the door and just as I expect she's dressed, minus her shoes. "I'll go," she says." I should go to the other room."

I catch her to me, fold her close, and kiss the hell out of her. Her resistance is short-lived, and she melts into me, kissing the hell out of me right back. "Why are you dressed?" I ask when our lips part. "We aren't even close to done with each other."

"I told you, I'm not good at the sex is just sex thing." Her resistance has returned, her hand pressing weakly against my chest. "I need to go."

There are reasons why I am a loner, a past I don't talk about, and history that taught me what is, or at least was, right for me, is to be alone. But I don't even hesitate when I say, "If this was just sex, Bella, I'd be with the waitress downstairs."

"Of course, it's just sex."

"Come on, baby, we both know—"

"Do you even realize what you're saying? When we get back—"

"We'll figure it out."

"Tyler, I'm your employee and you're"—she presses her lips together—"captive to what saves the company and people's jobs. I need to go. It's what's right for us both. Let me by, please."

Now my lips press together and tension knots in my shoulders, but I will not force myself on anyone. I release her. "If that's what you want, Bella." I back out of the doorway, and she walks past me and retrieves her boots, pulling them on where she stands before facing me, hands on her hips. Her hair is wild, sexy, well fucked, while she is not. Not yet. "I need the key to the other room," she states.

"My stuff is in that room Bella. I'll leave." I walk past her, and snatch up my shirt, pulling it on. Then fix my pants, and pull on my own boots. When I stand to leave, she's still where she was, hugging herself, watching me.

I close the distance between me and her and stand in front of her. "You feel as good as you taste. I won't forget that." I walk toward the door and pause, rotating to face her. "I can leave, Bella, right now, and go to my room, where you are not or I can stay and we can order pizza and fuck again."

Her chin dips and she presses her fingers to her forehead before she looks at me and asks, "What kind of pizza, and is there a spanking involved?"

LISA RENEE JONES

CHAPTER FORTY-FOUR

Bella

I wake to the ringing of my cellphone, only to realize I'm naked and pressed too close to Tyler. Actually, I'm curled around him from behind. My God, I not only stayed with him all night, I'm clinging to him like a fool, my hand on his hip. I try to shift away from him and Tyler catches my hand. "Where are you going?"

"My phone is ringing," I say, eager to escape this embarrassment. I'm spooning him. What girl does that to a guy? He does it to her.

"I couldn't give two fucks about your phone when you're naked, and your breasts are nuzzling my back," he says, and he catches my hand and shifts us so that I'm now holding his very large, very hard cock.

"Oh my God," I whisper.

"Just what every man wants to hear from his woman." He rolls to his back, one hand behind his head, the other closed around my hand on his cock.

"I'm not your woman, Tyler," I say.

He rolls us both to our sides facing each other, molding me close, his erection pressed between my legs. "You feel like my woman to me."

My chest tightens. "I don't like this game, Tyler."

He cups my face and tilts my gaze to his. "It's not a game."

"You have obligations and I'm your—" He presses inside me and I moan as he slides deep. "You are so hard."

"Glad you noticed," he says, squeezing my backside. "And I'm so fucking hard because I've been thinking about laying you across my lap and spanking you." He eases his cock back, almost pulling out of me.

And then thrusts hard.

I pant out a breath and stop fighting what is already in process. Maybe I'm taking everything way too seriously. And besides, he may never be inside me again, and he feels *so good*. He seems to sense my commitment to what we've started because he turns on his back and pulls me on top of him.

It's broad daylight and I'm riding him, and his eyes devour me like I'm the hottest woman he's ever known. He sits up as if he has to touch me, and cups my breasts, rocking with me, kissing me. And when we shatter, it's with him holding me just like this. "You're going to be the death of me, woman," he murmurs. He's still inside me when he scoots off the bed, stands up, and carries me to the bathroom. When we're all cleaned up, he sets me on the edge of the counter and presses his hands on either side of me, his mood shifting, darker, intense.

"Bella," he starts, and the grimness of his tone tells a story. It's time for a reality check for both of us. "I don't know what to do," he says, and I can feel his torment. "I don't want anything my father has forced on me."

The sincerity in his tone does a number on me and I press my hand to his face. "We're friends that had a moment, Tyler."

"We're not friends, Bella."

I blanch, stabbed by that statement when his hands come down on my knees. "I don't like how that simplifies what is going on between us. But yes, *of course,* we're friends, and that's what makes this different for me. 'We're friends' is not a statement I make about anyone I fuck, Bella."

"I get that, I do, but it doesn't change us really. We can still *be* friends and not sleep together. And I'm not leaving the company unless you decide you want me to. I just—I can't have this come out, or everyone...you know what they will think."

"I'm not going to let *us* hurt you, Bella. And why would I want you to leave? You're one of the best decisions I've ever made, and there is a boardroom of partners who would agree with me. I don't want any of what comes with my father's will. You have to know that."

"How damning is the case he threatened to take public? Are you sure it's as bad as you think?"

"Yes. It's bad. If it would have happened ten years later, or even five, I would have stopped it. I was a young buck trying to please my father. A father I should have hated at that point in my life."

"There has to be a way to deal with it and then go to court over the will."

"All I can do is everything I can do to stop this before I'm forced to marry. I have six months to act out a public engagement farce to make that happen."

Six months for him to date, sleep with, and devote himself to one woman who is not me. I'm queasy at this point.

My cellphone rings in the main room. "I really need to check that." I grab his wrist and glance at his watch, perfectly comfortable touching him at this point. *Too comfortable*, I think. "We only have an hour until our meeting," I add, and he helps me off the counter.

I grab the robe from behind the door, slip it on and run for my phone. I find it on the floor by the bed, no longer ringing, but with a cluster of text messages from Dash that seem to be about the studio.

I punch in Dash's autodial and sit down on the bed. "What's going on?"

"You still sleep like a rock. The studio head I didn't want to work with called me."

"He called you?"

"He did and we talked for over an hour. He's willing to meet all my terms and then some if we sign a letter of intent today, and up the money. He said he'd talk about that with you. He also said he'd come to you at your hotel. I think he wants to hold you captive so you don't go to the competition. Text him the time and address and he'll be there." At this point Tyler is wearing his pants, sitting next to me, trying to pick up pieces of the conversation. "I'm on it. How do you feel about this, Dash? Is this where you want to land?"

"How do *you* feel about it? What's your opinion?"

"I think the new studio head at our existing studio is going to screw you."

"Then make it happen," he says. "Let's seal this deal."

"Do you want us to meet with the existing studio just to be safe before we agree to anything?"

"Oh, that's right. 'We' means you and Tyler. He's there with you. How is that going?"

So very good and so very bad, I think, but what I say is, "It isn't yet. We haven't met with anyone. What do you think? Do we meet with both studios?"

"If you can get me a written document this morning, let's say adios to the new studio head and his dickhead attitude. After all, I do have a wedding to plan."

And so does Tyler, I think bitterly. "You do," I say. "Let's make all of this happen. Stay close to your phone. I'll need you to sign a document."

"I'll be around. Knock 'em dead, sis." He disconnects.

I shift toward Tyler. "The studio head he previously disliked called and offered him everything and the book, including more money, as long as we sign a letting of intent today."

"And he wants to take it?"

"He does. He seemed ready to make this happen. And the studio head is coming here. I need to text him a time. Do you want to do it in the suite at the table?"

Tyler leans across me and grabs the hotel phone from the nightstand. "I'll see if the hotel has a conference room we can use." He glances at his watch. "Tell him ten. It's seven now. In light of this new development, we need plenty of time to grab a bite and talk through our strategy."

"Agreed," I say and he makes the call, securing a conference room. With location and time in mind, I text the studio head, who confirms and agrees with the plan almost instantly. I set my phone down on the nightstand. "We're all set."

"I need to go grab my suitcases. Can you order us a carafe of coffee?"

"Of course," I say, but when he would move away, I catch his arm, halting his departure. "Tyler, I think we can go home tonight."

"We're going home Monday, baby. Unless you object, I'm keeping you for me this weekend."

Yes, please, I think, but I'm also not thinking logically. I'm fairly ready to admit most things I do with Tyler are a combination of hormones and emotions. "Do you think that's a good idea?"

"Hell, yes, I do," he assures me. "I want to stay the weekend. Do you?"

"I do, I just—"

He leans over and kisses me. "Then we're staying."

"But we fly home commercial," I counter. "When we head home, I need to just slip back into boss and employee mode. I just...I do."

"Okay. If I get you for the weekend, we'll keep our commercial flights home. Coffee, woman. I need coffee to get my bad cop juices flowing. Be a good cop and order."

I laugh and watch him pull on his shirt and shoes, and then head for the door. I order the coffee and breathe out. I'm really, really deeply invested emotionally in Tyler.

I am going to hurt when we get home. I'm going to hurt when I see the show with his new fiancée. I might have to leave the company. I don't know if I'll have a choice.

CHAPTER FORTY-FIVE

Bella

Tyler and I shower together, and I finish what I started last night on my knees, with him against the wall and his fingers twined in my hair. When it's over, he returns the favor, and leaves me trembling, my knees weak.

"You are better than any fantasy, baby," he tells me, kissing me all slow and sultry before we slip out of the now-cold water.

Fantasy.

I plant that word in my mind with a purpose. All of this is between me and him, is that and nothing more. I vow to spend the weekend enjoying the fantasy, and living in the moment, not my dread of what happens when we go home. Once we've dried off, our meeting time is creeping up on us and we quickly dress. In LA, business attire is on the casual side, and I opt for a sleeveless, emerald, form-fitting dress, with black heels.

Tyler dresses in a fitted, expensive gray suit that fits every defined muscle of his body to perfection. I don't miss that he has an extra edge of arrogance this morning, and I wonder if he packs a bit in a pocket to pull out when meeting with a possible opponent, as is the studio head. But I like this no-nonsense, make money and success, and take no names, Tyler. But he reminds me of all that awaits back home, just by existing. A realization I shake off. Right now is about Dash and his deal and nothing more.

Tyler's cellphone rings and he grabs it from the bathroom counter, where he's been tending his tie. "It's the hotel," he announces and then answers, "Tyler Hawk," and listens a moment, before he says, "We're on our way." He disconnects. "The conference room is ready. They'll bring him to us when he arrives. Ready, baby?"

The endearment does funny things to my insides and feels weird while we're in business mode, but I still like it. How can I *not* like it? "Let's go make this happen for my brother," I say.

He steps in front of me and kisses me. "Yes," he agrees. "Let's make it happen, Bella." His voice is a soft, sultry tone, and it's almost as if he's talking about us, not the meeting.

But then, I have fantasies of my own.

CHAPTER FORTY-SIX

Bella

We close the deal for Dash with a huge payday and everything my brother told me he wants in the contract.

The minute the studio head walks out of the conference room Tyler and I break out in a shared smile. "Call Dash," he says. "Then we're going to open a bottle of champagne. You just made all of us a huge payday, and turned your brother into one of the few writers who are as big as he's about to become."

"I know," I say, excitement bubbling inside me. "We closed the deal, Tyler. We did it."

"No, baby," he corrects. "*You* did this. I did nothing but come along for the ride because you knew when to use me."

Like we're using each other, I think, but firmly chide myself for going there.

"Call Dash, woman. He has to be on pins and needles."

"If I call Dash, he's going to want to celebrate. And I'll have to tell him I'm not coming home until Monday. He'll know I'm here with you."

"Tell him you have another deal you're working on."

"I'm with you. He's not stupid. He'll put two and two together."

"You're a grown adult, Bella. And he only knows what either of us tells him."

"And what will you say when he asks about us? Because I can tell from my conversations with him, he will."

"That you kicked ass and took names." He grabs the hotel phone. "I'm ordering us champagne."

I exhale and I dial Dash. I have to tell him the good news. That's just a must. "It's done," I say when he answers. "All of it. You got everything you wanted and a whole lot more money. Twenty-five percent more upfront and on the back end."

He whistles. "Damn, little sis. You are such a badass."

"You're the badass. You're the only reason any of this is happening. I'm so happy for you, Dash. And also, plan your wedding!"

"We're already talking about October in Aspen, right when the leaves change. What do you think?"

"I think it's perfect."

"Waffle day to celebrate? I'll get the champagne."

"I'm not coming back until Monday after a meeting," I say, promising myself I'll try to find a meeting so I'm not lying. I add a real truth to make myself feel better. "I prefer to wrap up more than one thing when I'm here, so I don't have to come often."

He's silent a moment. "Is Tyler with you?"

"He is," I confess quickly, trying not to make a big deal out of it. "He was a big help in the meeting. You should probably call him when you get a chance."

"Is he there now?"

"Yes. We're still in the hotel conference room. I couldn't wait to call you."

"Let me talk to him, Bella."

"Okay," I say, but it's not okay. Dash is going to say something personal, something about me. Tyler is now sitting on the table beside me. Lips pressed together, I offer the phone to him, a warning in my eyes.

He touches my face and mouths, "I got this," and places the phone to his ear. "Congrats, man. You are the man. The Hollywood man, now. This is solid. It's not going to fall apart like last time."

He listens a moment. "Yeah, well, I played bad cop to Bella's good cop, because she had the foresight to see that as necessary. But she barely needed me." He listens another moment and pushes off the table. "It's not our first rodeo. We've worked together for years, often one-on-one. Why are you coming at me now?"

My heart starts to race, and I push to my feet and away from the table, motioning for Tyler to hand me the phone. He waves me off. "I'm aware of what she means to you," he says, continuing his chat with my brother. "I happen to value her as an employee." His jaw tics. "Don't go there, man." He listens a minute and then hands me the phone. "He hung up."

"What did he say to you?" I ask.

"Not to fuck his sister." He scrubs a rough hand over his jaw and unbuttons his jacket, settling his hands on his hips. "Let's go get that champagne."

"He brought up Allison, didn't he?"

"He did, but I can't blame him. If you were my sister, I'd do the same. Seriously, baby, let's go get that champagne. We need to celebrate."

I step in front of him and press my hands to his waist. "I'm sorry."

"Don't be. I'm the one who crossed about ten lines with you, Bella." His hand settles on my side. "Don't resign when we get back. I will not be the reason you walk away from all you've worked for. I'd already planned to talk to you about becoming a partner if you made this deal happen. And before you say anything, I hired you. Your success is a sense of pride for me."

"You want me to be partner?" I ask, and I can't help it, I'm fearful this has something to do with us—this weekend—not me.

"What did I just see in your eyes, Bella?" He grimaces and doesn't wait for my reply, his hand moving to my lower back and molding me closer. "Damn it, don't go there. Don't think this opportunity is about this—about *us*—when you worked for it. I can show you the paperwork I drew up before I ever touched you."

"I don't even have a secretary, but you're offering me partner?"

"I approved one six months ago, Bella."

My brows dip. "Was it that long ago?"

"Yes. I'll hire one for you if that's what it takes to make you feel appreciated. I just thought you'd want to pick the person."

"I do. I mean...partner is big."

"Yeah. So is this deal you just made happen. Anyone else who achieved what you have would be partner. And not many achieved what you have, Bella. You get that, right?"

"I've worked hard. You're right. I deserve this. I'm happy."

"Good. Can we go celebrate now? Champagne in the room and then I'll take you to dinner."

"I don't think that's a good idea. We might be seen and—"

He kisses me hard and fast, but thoroughly, and says, "I want to say I don't give two fucks, but you just questioned your success over us. I'm not going to let anyone else do the same. We'll order in. And go to a dark movie, if you want. I'll even see a chick flick for you."

"Okay, now you're talking. You had me at chick flick, but we can watch something else. But—" I hold up a finger. "We have all weekend. We're watching *Pretty Woman* with Julia Roberts at some point in the room."

"*Black Adam* wins for tonight. *Pretty Woman* tomorrow night."

I smile and we both grab our things to head to the room. And it almost, *almost,* feels like we're a couple.

LISA RENEE JONES

CHAPTER FORTY-SEVEN

Bella

I have so much fun with Tyler. When he's not in "Tyler Hawk" mode, but just Tyler, he's funny and charming. But the wall is still there. Beyond things like favorite movies, books, and food, he uses sex to avoid anything deeper. But as we step on the plane super early Monday morning, I think it's for the best. I'm kind of a wreck, but I try to hide it from him.

I hide behind my work, telling him I have to catch up on the plane. When lunch arrives, and I'm forced to set my MacBook aside, I hyperfocus on my food.

"Bella," he says, compelling me to look at him.

"Yes?"

"Don't shut me out."

"We have to go back to normal."

"Is this normal?"

"For now," I say and motion to his food. "Eat. We both know you eat enough for an army." I refocus on my food and he eventually gives in and picks up his fork.

When we land and everyone begins to deplane, he refuses to let me exit, facing me and caging me by the window. Damn him for smelling so good the entire flight and for wearing a snug T-shirt that hugs his perfect upper torso and makes me want to do the same.

"I'm going to stay with you tonight," he announces, as if the decision is made. "We'll talk and figure this out."

My heart skips a beat but I manage a solid, "No. No, you are not. It's done. I'm not good at *this* kind of thing, as we've discussed, so just let me go lick my wounds and I'll see you at work tomorrow."

"Damn it, Bella. It doesn't have to be like this."

"On some level, you know better, and you'll get that when we're apart. Exit the plane, Tyler, before I get emotional and make a fool of myself in front of everyone and *my boss*."

His jaw tics and seconds crawl by before he says, "Have it your way." He turns away from me and waits for the aisle to clear.

We walk to the baggage claim in silence and he insists on getting my bag for me. "I have a car waiting for us."

"I'll catch a cab."

"Don't be silly, Bella. I'll give you a ride."

"No," I say. "I don't need a ride."

"I'm walking you to your cab then."

"I've got it." I turn and start walking.

He catches up to me, stubbornly keeping pace.

Once I'm in the cab line, he's in the cab line with me. When it's my turn to load into a car, he pulls me into his arms, cups my face, and says, "I have to do this."

"Someone could see us, Tyler. What if—"

His mouth slants over mine, and he kisses me like he will never kiss me again. Because he won't. When he releases me, he says, "I'll see you soon," and then strides away.

Watching him leave creates a biting ache in my belly. I have too many feelings for that man for my own good. Because the only place it got me was alone again.

CHAPTER FORTY-EIGHT

Bella

I don't even think about going to the office. It's nearly five anyway, and I walk into my lonely home and wish again for a dog. I really need a furry friend. That's not in the cards right now, not when my career feels up in the air. I make a pot of coffee, sit down at my island and start checking in with clients. I feel like I'm days behind on everything.

By seven, I'm in the bathtub with a pint of ice cream next to me. The idea of going to work tomorrow kills me, but I did this to myself. I hate what I've done to my work life. I will never go to the office and not worry about how what happened between me and Tyler affects my career. If that kiss was seen by anyone, I'd be ruined. Not that I think it was. But so would Tyler. He can't afford an employee-boss scandal right now.

All things lessen with time, I tell myself, but I still take a huge bite of ice cream.

CHAPTER FORTY-NINE

I stand at the window of Gavin's office, staring out at the city and listening to him talk without really seeing what is before me or hearing what he's saying. "Are you listening to me, Tyler?"

I rotate to find him leaning on the edge of his desk. Gavin is my age, early thirties, a smooth-talking ladies' man, with sandy brown hair, soaring ambition, and skills to match.

"The contract is fine. I read it. It protects me, and the money is high enough that no one is going to want to run their mouth and lose it."

"I need the list of women you want to be considered."

I laugh without humor and eye the ceiling. "That's not so simple."

"What the hell are you talking about?"

"Do you know Bella Bailey?"

"Of course, I know Bella. She's gorgeous and successful. What man wouldn't know her? Oh, fuck. You're in bed with her. Holy hell, Tyler. After Allison—"

"It's not the same. I have feelings for her." I speak those words effortlessly, and that says a lot about where I stand right now.

"I think the ground just shook. Since when do you have feelings for *anyone*?"

"Now," I say. "And if I do this fake fiancée thing, I will lose her."

"If you don't, you lose a shit ton of money and the company. The company being the big one here, because everyone attached to the company, me included, could end up screwed over if leadership flies south. We're talking a lot of lives here, Tyler. Hundreds of employees."

"What if I talked to Bella? Her mother was Alice, from Alice Shopping Network. Her father is Victor Bailey."

"The NASCAR driver?"

"Yes. She's swimming in money. She doesn't need mine. And I trust her."

"She's perfect, except for one thing. She obviously values creating a life and a career for herself because no one here knows about her mother. And I sure didn't know about her father. The minute it's discovered that you two are together, she's ruined. It will be assumed she slept her way to the top. If you have feelings for her, convince her the rest of this shit is as fake as it is, and don't fuck the other chick. But you cannot be caught with Bella. There's small print you need to know about."

"What small print?"

"If anything about this 'marriage' is deemed for show, you lose everything. I'm guessing there's a PI who will be following you. You have to assume you will be watched."

"Of course, I will be. And as for Bella, the other woman is just never going to fly with her. And you're right. Her career matters to her. Hell, she's up for partner, and that was on the table before we ever got involved. She just closed a major deal for her brother, Dash. I can't take that from her."

"Then get a list. You have fifteen months to screw this up, or six months plus a short marriage to end this. Once you inherit, it's done."

"What about the company? What will anyone know?"

"Nothing. You're the crowned CEO and majority stockholder until you're not. I'll spare you the details unless you want to hear them, but technically you inherited the stock and maintain your current role of CEO, with stipulations. As of today, you are no longer in an acting role. You're the real deal. Notifications have been sent out to all partners. With your permission, I'll send a formal notice to the clients of the firm."

"Yes. Do it. We're done here. I need to think." I walk toward the door.

"Get me the list," he calls out.

I lift a hand and say nothing.

There is only one name on my list, and that's Bella, as impossible as that seems right now.

CHAPTER FIFTY

I work late, buried in a multitude of things I should have handled days ago. It's almost ten o'clock when I leave the office and intend to drive home. Instead, I drive to Bella's house and sit outside, talking myself out of going inside. My cellphone rings with Gavin's number, almost as if he knows where I'm at and he wants to check me.

"Yeah," I answer.

"I hope like hell you aren't with Bella. You will ruin her. You will ruin yourself. You will ruin lives. Let me be a little clearer: she is not good for you if she ruins your lives and those of others. Get me my list."

"I get it. Did you call for anything I need to hear?"

"We both know you needed to hear that. I'll come get the list. Where are you?"

"I'll get it to you when I get home. Goodbye, Gavin."

"Wait," he says. "What was that bullshit your father said, about you finding out more about him, and what he was into? Paraphrasing, of course."

Holy hell, I think. I haven't even thought about that portion of my father's letter at all. "Dierk will handle it."

"All right. Let me know if you need me. And I'll be looking for—"

I hang up before he can say "list" and dial Dierk.

"Tyler," he greets. "What do you have for me?"

I give him the rundown on the family involved in the legal case, the situation with the will, and the warning from my father about his behavior I'd soon learn about.

"Find a way to get me out of this. And if you can't do that, find a way to ensure I keep the Allen family on a leash."

"They're powerful. That's a big order."

"I'm powerful, more so when I inherit five hundred million. Get me something to control them. And I need to know what my father was into. I need to head it off."

"That I can do. More soon."

We disconnect and I'm still sitting outside Bella's home. She's under my skin and that's a problem. Gavin isn't wrong. I have to control this situation or people will get hurt. Hell, convicted criminals might get free just because our firm touched their cases if it comes out we withheld evidence for the Allen family. But I'm not going to stay away from Bella. I've never felt like I couldn't stay away from a woman, but my present location sums up where I stand. I want her, and I want her badly. She's the first woman, since—since a long time ago that I've allowed myself to have feelings for. And I didn't even allow this to happen. She took me off guard when not much does.

My fingers thrum on the dash. *Control*, I think. I need it. And I don't have it when Bella has it and right now, she does. There's only one way to handle this. I need to fuck her about a thousand times and get her out of my system. I don't want to hurt Bella, but I have to think about all the hundreds of employees, too. No more of this emotional bullshit.

No more.

I know what I have to do and I punch in Gavin's number. "I need some changes to that contract."

CHAPTER FIFTY-ONE

Tyler

I meet with Gavin the next morning and review the contract. "You sure this is how you want to handle this?"

"Positive," is my only reply. "And now I have a company to run." I leave him staring after me, relatively speechless. He knows me. When I'm this sold on something, he needs to let it ride.

But he doesn't. I'm at the door when he says, "For the record. You're fucking yourself, man, but it's your call."

I don't turn around. I exit the office with no intention of running into Bella, who will not want to see me, but that's exactly what I do. I'm barely two steps from Gavin's office when she appears. She gasps softly at the sight of me, and we're so close, we almost run into each other. I can smell her perfume and I remember exactly how she tastes. Like honey. Like *my woman*. And damn it to hell, I want to pull her to me and kiss the fuck out of her. She's in a black, figure-hugging skirt, with a blue silk blouse that brightens the blue of her eyes.

Her skin is creamy and perfect. Her lips are painted pink, full and un-kissed when they need to be kissed. But all my lust-laden thoughts don't outweigh the obvious. She's outside Gavin's office and my suspicion flares. If he ran his mouth, friend or no friend, he's gone. "What are you doing here?"

She holds up a folder. "The contract came. The legal team lead said Gavin would be the best person to have look at a few things. He wasn't answering my calls so I walked over."

Of course, she did. Because she gets the job done. "Do I need to look at it?"

"Not right now. I already worked it over pretty hard. Once Gavin goes through it, I'll make sure you approve it before it goes to Dash."

"How worrisome are the concerns?"

"Not huge, but the wording is a bit tricky, so I want to be sure there isn't a loophole or two hiding in plain sight."

"Smart. He's eager. Whoever drafted that contract worked the weekend to do it."

"Yes," she says. "I thought the same thing, but Hollywood goes hot to cold fast. I want the deal done and done now."

"Agreed." I hesitate. "Bella—"

"Don't," she says softly. "Please. I'm good. I'm motivated this morning and excited for us and my brother. I'll email you when I'm done with Gavin with an update."

Email me. Before this, it would have been a phone call. "Call me. It's what you would have done in the past. Nothing has changed."

Her teeth scrape her bottom lip. "Right. Of course. Nothing has changed." She cuts her stare and steps around me. I turn and watch her disappear into Gavin's office. We need to talk, me and Bella. And before this day is over, we will.

CHAPTER FIFTY-TWO

Bella

I walk into my front door and lean on the hard surface and exhale with relief.

Somehow, I survived this day, but it was hard. Seeing Tyler first thing outside Gavin's office was awkward and emotional. And Gavin was weird, too. He kept staring at me, almost as if he knew something he should not know, but that's crazy. Tyler is a private person. I don't believe he would talk about me to anyone. My cellphone rings and I snake it out of my jacket to find Dash calling.

"Allie and I are on our way over. We got you a little celebratory gift. We just wanted to make sure you were home."

I grimace at the idea of company despite how much I love them both, but then again, maybe company is exactly what I need. "I'm here. I just got here."

"See you in thirty to forty-five minutes."

"Perfect. I have time to change and get comfy."

We disconnect and my doorbell rings. I frown because I'm not sure who would be here. Perhaps this time I really do have a package delivery, or a neighbor visiting with a package meant for me.

I grab the things I've set on the floor, place them on the entry table, then open the door. I blanch and my heart lurches at the sight of Tyler standing there. His suit jacket is gone, and his white shirt sleeves are rolled up to display powerful forearms. He smells so good I want to lick him all over and I hate him for stirring such thoughts in me. "What are you doing here?"

He lifts a folder in his hand. "I need to go over some contractual information with you."

My eyes go wide. Damn it, I must have missed something in the contract and Dash is on his way over here. "What is it?" I ask urgently.

"Can I come in?"

I hesitate but I nod and back up, allowing his entry. I shut the door and lean on it again. He turns to face me. "Let's go sit."

No, I think, but what I say is, "Right. Let's go sit. The kitchen table will be good."

He motions me forward. "Lead the way."

I move ahead of him, my knees weak with the heaviness of his eyes on my progress. The walk across the living room feels far and wide, but finally, we reach my table, the smaller one off the actual kitchen rather than the large dining room table. I stand on one side and wait for him to sit. His lips quirk as if he knows I'm waiting to choose my seat, based on where he places himself. He goes opposite of me, and we both settle in. The table is smaller than it seems normally, and we are closer than I intend.

"I thought this was better done away from the office." He slides the folder in front of me.

I can only assume he means due to distractions.

I open it and stare down at a document that reads: *This agreement is between two parties, Tyler Hawk and Bella Bailey.*

I blink and my gaze jerks to Tyler's. "What is this?"

"We're not going to stay away from each other, Bella. I'm going to be followed by a PI, looking for me to screw up. If I touch you, and you are not my fiancée, I lose everything. The company loses everything."

I'm shell-shocked. "So wait, *I'm* the problem here?"

"That's not what I'm saying at all. I trust you. I know you won't screw me, Bella. I need to trust the person I call my fiancée. And that gives us time to fuck each other out of our systems"

He might as well have stabbed me right in the heart. "Right. Because it's all about sex." He opens his mouth to speak and I hold up a hand, anger churning in my belly. "Everyone will think I slept my way to the top. No." I shut the folder and slide it to him. "I don't need to fuck you out of my system, Tyler. You just finished this for me."

"I'm not going to let this screw you, Bella. I want you to open a film division for Hawk Legal. We'll set it up as another company. Additionally, I'll ensure your salary is double, as you will head that division. Furthermore, I know money isn't an issue for you, but this is a mammoth-sized commitment. When I inherit, there is a substantial payout for you in the contract. I do not want to take advantage of you, Bella, but I need you by my side. And I *want* you by my side."

I swear I can feel my heart shattering into pieces and then exploding into anger. My voice quakes and I say, "The crazy part is I would have done this for you, as a friend. For you and the company because you know—I just would have. And I didn't need a contract to go away. I learned the hard way that love is rare and my parents were lucky to have it. I don't want to get married. I don't want to fall in love and be burned by nastiness like this." I lose control and throw the folder at him, before standing up. "I'm done. We're done. And, no, I'm not going to quit my job. I'm going to stay and congratulate your new fiancée on her future happiness. Everybody will think I mean her life with you, but I'll mean her big payday."

"Bella—"

He is on his feet rounding the table. "No." I point at him and back away. "Don't even think about touching me."

He curses and scrubs his jaw, and somehow, he manages to look tormented, like I really matter to him. How many women has he made think they mattered to him when they were just sex? "Forget the contract," he says. "Just do this with me. Date me. Marry me. This isn't how I wanted this to work out. I thought we'd both have the freedom—"

"To fuck each other out of our systems? *Leave, Tyler.*"

My doorbell rings and I say, "That will be Dash and Allie."

"Of course, it is," he says. "Now I have to leave, but this isn't over. We are not over."

"We are so over, Tyler. You insulted me, and tried to pay me off. I feel like a whore. You made me feel like a whore."

"Bella," he breathes out. "God, woman. I don't think—" The doorbell rings again, and he huffs out a breath. "I'm going." He rotates on his heel and strides toward the door.

I follow him, and why on Earth do I want to scream for him to stop? Why do I hurt so badly at the idea of him leaving? I reach the edge of the foyer as he opens the door to face Dash and Allie.

"What the hell are you doing here, Tyler?" Dash demands.

"Ask your sister," is all Tyler says, and then he disappears out into the hallway.

Dash and Allie step into the foyer, and Allie is holding a Golden Retriever puppy. I've wanted a Golden Retriever since I was a kid, but my mom was busy, and often traveled all over the place with my father. I just couldn't have a dog. In my mind, when I think of getting a dog, it's a Golden.

"Surprise!" Allie says, while Dash counters with, "What the fuck is going on, Bella?

I burst into tears.

The End...for now

Tyler & Bella's story continues in Sweet Sinner which is out very soon! Pre-order now! Also, did you love Allie and Dash? Their story is told in the Necklace Trilogy which is complete and available now! Keep reading for an excerpt from their first book :)

https://www.lisareneejones.com/tyler--bella-duet.html

***

WANT MORE FROM ME? Check out my freebie and upcoming release!

***

FREE BOOK!

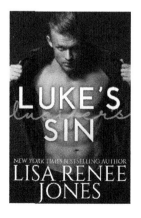

237

https://bookhip.com/TGSXDKM

***

UPCOMING RELEASE: THE PARTY IS OVER (LILAH LOVE)

Sometimes a girl just has to get stabby... Lilah has sworn she's done with that side of her personality. Then again, maybe not. The Party Is Over is the eighth book in the Lilah Love series, start the series for FREE with Murder Notes! Series information here:

https://www.lisareneejonesthrillers.com/the-lilah-love-series.html

***

TURN THE PAGE FOR AN EXCERPT FROM THE NECKLACE TRILOGY!

THE NECKLACE TRILOGY

A necklace delivered to the wrong Allison: me. I'm the wrong Allison.

That misplaced gift places a man in my path. A man who instantly consumes me and leads me down a path of dark secrets and intense passion.

Dash Black is a famous, bestselling author, but also a man born into wealth and power. He owns everything around him, every room he enters. He owns me the moment I meet him. He seduces me oh so easily and reveals another side of myself I dared not expose. Until him. Until this intense, wonderful, tormented man shows me another way to live and love. I melt when he kisses me. I shiver when he touches me. And I like when he's in control, especially when I thought I'd never allow anyone that much power over me ever again.

We are two broken people who are somehow whole when we are together, but those secrets—his, and yes, I have mine as well—threaten to shatter all that is right and make it wrong.

FIND OUT MORE ABOUT THE NECKLACE TRILOGY HERE:

https://www.lisareneejones.com/necklace-trilogy.html

***

READ AN EXCERPT

"I'll lick you anywhere you want to be licked if you just say please."

I'm really, truly a rather shy person and no one has ever spoken to me so boldly as Dash has this night, but I'm different with Dash I'm starting to realize. More comfortable in my own skin. I just can't find it in me to hide from this or him. "What about where I want to kiss *you*?"

"Where do you want to kiss me?" he asks, squeezing my backside.

"Everywhere," I assure him.

His lips curve and he says, "Is that right?"

"Oh yes, but you resist me, Dash Black."

"I assure you, Allison, I'm not resisting." Somehow him calling me Allison in this moment is more intimate than Allie, and I don't know why. "I want nothing more than your hands and mouth on my body," he says. "But you'll have to allow me to kiss you everywhere first."

ALSO BY LISA RENEE JONES

THE INSIDE OUT SERIES
If I Were You
Being Me
Revealing Us
His Secrets*
Rebecca's Lost Journals
The Master Undone*
My Hunger*
No In Between
My Control*
I Belong to You
All of Me*

THE SECRET LIFE OF AMY BENSEN
Escaping Reality
Infinite Possibilities
Forsaken
Unbroken*

CARELESS WHISPERS
Denial
Demand
Surrender

WHITE LIES
Provocative
Shameless

TALL, DARK & DEADLY / WALKER SECURITY
Hot Secrets
Dangerous Secrets
Beneath the Secrets
Deep Under

Pulled Under
Falling Under
Savage Hunger
Savage Burn
Savage Love
Savage Ending
When He's Dirty
When He's Bad
When He's Wild
Luke's Sin
Luke's Touch
Luke's Revenge

LILAH LOVE
Murder Notes
Murder Girl
Love Me Dead
Love Kills
Bloody Vows
Bloody Love
Happy Death Day
The Party Is Over

DIRTY RICH
Dirty Rich One Night Stand
Dirty Rich Cinderella Story
Dirty Rich Obsession
Dirty Rich Betrayal
Dirty Rich Cinderella Story: Ever After
Dirty Rich One Night Stand: Two Years Later
Dirty Rich Obsession: All Mine
Dirty Rich Betrayal: Love Me Forever
Dirty Rich Secrets

THE FILTHY TRILOGY
The Bastard
The Princess
The Empire

THE NAKED TRILOGY
One Man
One Woman
Two Together

THE BRILLIANCE TRILOGY
A Reckless Note
A Wicked Song
A Sinful Encore

NECKLACE TRILOGY
What If I Never
Because I Can
When I Say Yes

eBook only

ABOUT LISA RENEE JONES

New York Times and *USA Today* bestselling author Lisa Renee Jones writes dark, edgy fiction including the highly acclaimed *Inside Out* series and the crime thriller *The Poet*. Suzanne Todd (producer of Alice in Wonderland and Bad Moms) on the *Inside Out* series: *Lisa has created a beautiful, complicated, and sensual world that is filled with intrigue and suspense.*

Prior to publishing, Lisa owned a multi-state staffing agency that was recognized many times by The Austin Business Journal and also praised by the Dallas Women's Magazine. In 1998 Lisa was listed as the #7 growing women-owned business in Entrepreneur Magazine. She lives in Colorado with her husband, a cat that talks too much, and a Golden Retriever who is afraid of trash bags.

Printed in Great Britain
by Amazon